To Be Claimed

Book Four

WILLOW WINTERS

WALL STREET JOURNAL & USA TODAY BESTSELLING AUTHOR

From USA TODAY Bestselling Author Willow Winters comes a fast paced and sizzling fated mates standalone romance in her best selling paranormal world.

Fate never prepared me for seeing my mate with the claiming mark of my enemy.

She doesn't know she's my mate. She doesn't feel the burning pull between us. The desperate need to love and be loved by me as I feel raging inside me.

None of this should have happened this way.

I don't know how she came to be his, but I'll slowly torture him if his claim has broken my mate's ability to feel our bond.
The war has already begun and when the dust settles she will be mine.

I can't imagine an existence without her ... and my greatest fear is that it's all too late.

Broken Fate is a complete standalone. You can read it without reading anything else or enjoy it before or after the Wounded Kiss trilogy.

BROKEN
FATE

PROLOGUE

JUDE

E ven if my heart is racing, I blend in perfectly, just as I've been trained to do. The mud masks my scent and they have no fucking clue I've been watching them for hours. All the while an anxiousness fights against my instincts. Devin, my Alpha, tasked me with recon to get a good look at the enemy and their defenses. They targeted us first, threatened the Alpha mate... so they have this coming. I had my suspicions, but I never could have known how damn weak Shadow's pack is. It's unfortunate that addiction has destroyed their wolves. It's more than obvious with their lazy sparring in between swigs of whiskey and snorts of cocaine. The arrogance that is Shadow, their Alpha, finally surfaced a few minutes ago with his young mate, and I hadn't realized I could be shocked further.

I anticipated feeling pity for this pack, like I have so many others that have young pups and difficulties my pack can only imagine. Until last week, we were only a small pack of males—not a single one of us had found our mate. With the damage fate raised us with before bringing the Shadow Falls pack together, I thought it best there was no one to share this life with. So when it comes to other packs, ones with children, I have mercy.

Not this time. The longer I observe, the angrier I become. It's a little too close to what was once my home.

The Alpha mate, a petite and rather thin brunette with slicked-back hair, smirks as she kicks the two pups to the side. "Move and wait your turn," she speaks loud enough for the entire camp to hear. Although, I'm unsure the pups understand. They're both in poor health and have poor hygiene. As are the half a dozen adults sharing the charred meal of venison around the open flames. With torn jeans and simple shirts stained with blood and dirt, the elders of the pack pay no mind to anything apart from their meal. Merely pushed to the side, the two pups seem to gather up energy to continue their efforts, desperate to get at the bones the males are tossing to the side around the fire pit.

I would be shocked if the pups were hers, although no other adult seems to care. Two men glance back over their shoulder before scooting down the makeshift bench to provide a spot for their Alpha mate. The two other women don't spare the pups a glance, even with the faint yelp from the smallest.

It's sickening to watch. My mind races with possibilities that the two are runts and are practically abandoned, or that the mother passed bringing them here.

Taking stock of the women gathered around the fire, I'm not given any clues to the pups, only to their addiction and poor health. I'm surprised their bones aren't poking through the thin flesh covering their frail bodies.

A strangled sob from a hut on the left of the clearing captures my attention. It also catches Shadow's mate's attention, and she rises instantly, standing so quickly five of the six pack members around the fire watch her carefully. Not the Alpha though. Shadow doesn't bother looking up from his food. "Leave her alone."

"Why is that bitch even allowed to breathe the same air as me?" she hisses at her Alpha. Shadow blended into the pack before, but her comment raises his hackles, his spine stiffens as he straightens his shoulders toward her. There's a menacing dominance about him, and the other men still, waiting and watching.

His cold eyes finally meet hers as he sneers, "Because she's pregnant with my pup." My heart beats once out of turn as I take in the scene. My emotions are far too high from the sight before me.

Her nose scrunches in disgust. "That's your fault for taking a mate that wasn't yours." I suppress the growl growing in my chest. A mate is for life, yet he's taken two. One of which isn't his true mate? As the scene unfolds, my wolf paces faster and presses against my chest. So much is wrong, but holding my wolf back has never been a challenge before.

Shadow rises from his seat on the log bench around the fire and stalks to his mate. She stands defiantly before cowering slightly, seeming to resign herself to her fate. His hand whips through the air, slaps her cheek, and busts her lip open. The smack makes one of the other women flinch, but the men don't move. No one says a word as the Alpha mate lands hard on her side in the dirt. I feel bile rise up my throat, but I stay still and will my disgust down.

"Don't you fucking question me." The rest of the pack continues to eat while they watch with little interest. It must be a common occurrence. Again, I get the feeling that it's all too close to what my life was once like for me to keep my wits about me. If my wolf's reaction is anything to go by, I shouldn't be here alone. I don't trust myself not to act.

"And when you finally get the pup you wanted?" She looks up at him with daggers, brushing her cheek but staying on the ground. A moan of pain echoes through the camp from the hut, but no one bothers to turn their attention away from their Alphas' feud. Inside, my wolf muffles a howl of agony at the sound from the hut.

She's not well and my wolf begs me to save her and the pups.

"Then you can do what you want with her." He murmurs the words casually as he retakes his seat. A cruel smile forms on his mate's thin lips as she rises and takes a seat next to him, once again kicking one of the pups before she sits. Pure evil washes off her body in waves. A sickness rises inside of me as I gather her intent for Shadow's pregnant mate.

Questions gather as I watch them eat in relative silence until the pained cry interrupts them with nothing but annoyance.

"Someone drag that bitch out here and shove some food down her throat." Two wolves rise at the command from their Alpha, but with a quick glance at each other, one sits back down and continues ripping meat off the bone to gorge himself. I watch the other take long strides to the dirty hut and disappear for a moment before dragging out a woman by her hair. Her feet barely touch the ground.

My heart stops and all the air leaves my lungs. Her brunette hair is matted, her dull skin is covered with dirt, and her belly is swollen with Shadow's child. She whimpers as the wolf roughly shoves her down on her knees in front of the fire. A fury of rage boils inside of me.

I clench my fists and resist the urge to barrel down the hill and rip this pathetic pack apart. A snarl fumes in my chest, but I leave it there to flame the rage burning inside me. I watch as she stumbles in his grasp and sobs from the pain he's causing her. My wolf fights against my firmly planted feet. Frozen, afraid of what I'd do if I dared to move, I barely breathe until his hands are off her. I can't break the secure hold I have on my body. If I move an inch, fuck, even if I breathe too deeply, I'll let my beast out and devour as many of the useless wolves below me that I can.

But I'll fail.

Although they're weak, there are far too many of them for me to defeat. I'd make a dent in their numbers, but I will fail. My knuckles turn white as I clench my fists. The blood rushes in my ears as my heart pounds with turmoil.

I need to get a hold of Devin, but I can't leave her. It feels as though a thousand spikes are tearing through me, splintering my very being as I watch her suffer while I stay hidden in the shadows.

My body shakes with anger and a sense of failure and weakness. I struggle with the need to go to her, to my mate, to save her from the fucking nightmare she's living. I know she is my mate. There is no denying this pull. My wolf claws at me to be free, but I push him back, refusing to let him have the vengeance he so desperately wants.

Mine. My heart frantically beats in my chest as my wolf rages.

Soon. I tell my wolf and it's the only thing that keeps me sane in this moment.

I refuse to look away from her as I make a promise to my

wolf who whines in agony. Soon we'll go to her. We'll destroy this pack and make sure they suffer. Soon our mate will bear the mark of my claim to her. My gaze focuses on the silver scar on her neck as anger brews inside of me. How dare he claim what's mine. I'll kill Shadow and claim my mate if it's the last thing I ever do.

CHAPTER 1

LENA

I bear down and wince at another hard kick to my ribs. It's only slight pain, but I can't help the reaction. My little pup is so strong. His tiny foot pushes against my stomach and I gently place my hand against the print to feel him. The warmth and content that flow through me are all that keep me going. My lips curl up with a small smile as his foot disappears. Although it hurts, I love the feeling of him moving and stretching his legs. When I don't feel him, I worry; he can kick me all day long if he'd like. I'll take the pain and discomfort to know he's well.

A rousing in the distance steals my attention and raises my hackles. I wish I could hum a song I vaguely remember from my mother so my pup can hear my voice, but I'm far too afraid. I don't want them to hear me. It's best when they just forget I'm here. That's when it's safest for me. Swallowing thickly, I try to keep my heart from racing. It takes every ounce of energy in me to stay calm during days like these. Days when the shipment comes in and the pack partakes. So long as I'm quiet and stay inside, they forget me, and that's when I'm safest. I've learned to never try to run. The hut, although falling apart, is a sanctuary for me. No one wishes to be here.

The chill of the night creeps through the holes in the mud bricks and I huddle under the tattered blanket to protect myself from the breeze drifting through. I'm intent on simply surviving for the sake of my pup. The clay floor is bare and cold, yet it helps my swelling. I'll take this if it means I can be left alone. I want to be as far from them as I can.

Right now, I'm safer than I was before I carried the Alpha's child, but I know my days are numbered. I want to stay out of sight and out of mind for as long as I can. My mate has ruined me and the proud wolf I once was. I'm thankful that fate sent him another to bear the brunt of who he is. She was made for him, enjoying him and his dark ways. It offers me a reprieve.

I don't belong here, and I wish I didn't belong to him. The only good he's ever given me is to let me be alone in this cramped shelter. He made me watch as his new mate pleased him, made me sleep on the floor of the same room while he gave her attention and care he'd never given me. I'm grateful she convinced him to leave me alone here, but I'm terrified to sleep. She's come multiple times in the night while I've been pretending to sleep. Each time he's come up behind her and told her to leave me alone. I suppose that means I owe him a bit of gratitude.

She doesn't want me to carry his pup. I know she wishes me dead.

It's only a matter of time. She'll either defy Shadow and come to kill me in my sleep, or once my baby is born she'll end my life and no one will bother to stop her. I know this is true, yet I no longer fear it. There's a challenge buried inside of me. It does bring me grave sadness, knowing my child will be born into this. I have a plan though. Once I've delivered my pup, I'll run. I won't stop. I need to get my baby out of here. I will. That's the last hope I have. I'll do my best to fight them off and run as fast as I can. It may be the last chance I ever get, but I cling to the hope that I can try to free us one more time before I take my last breath.

I'll save my child in a way my parents couldn't save me.

Suppressing the hum of an almost forgotten lullaby, I rub my belly and remember how I used to dream of the day my mate would come and take me from my pack. The seers told me my mate would be an Alpha. They told me he would need me to create a worthy pack and to maintain strong ties with his previous pack so that they would join together and be an unstoppable force. They said a war was coming and I would bring a way for victory and peace. They told me lies. They filled my head with a fantasy that I was compelled to agree to. For the best of everyone else.

I remember the first time I saw Shadow. I remember my heart swelling with hope. The hope that my Alpha would take me away, make me his, and together we would do good in this world. I anticipated feeling a pull to my mate. The pull my pack always told me I'd feel. Like gravity didn't exist and your soul was meant to merge with the other. The heat that would come and the need to be held by my mate. My sister told me it was like an electric spark and magnetic force that got stronger as you got closer to your mate. Like you were so physically drawn to that person that air no longer existed.

Shadow said he felt it. Felt the need to give me everything, to make me happy, and give me all his love. It's not what I felt. There was something there, but it wasn't what they told me it would be.

We were alone in the woods with the full moon hanging above us, as it is supposed to be. Merida arranged our meeting. My sister was full of hopes and dreams back then. She was ecstatic that we were going to be in the same pack. That together we would raise a family of wolves that could rival any other pack. I followed her into the darkness. I trusted that Shadow's pull to me was enough, even if I didn't feel a great pull to him. I let him claim me that night while Rayne claimed my sister.

The memory of that night brings a chill over my body,

and my breath comes up short. Another holler from outside brings me back to the present. My fingers brush against his mark and my eyes close tightly remembering how much it hurt. My legs tremble, remembering the burn that scorched my entire body. It took hours to go away.

If I could go back, I'd never be claimed. I'd run from my mate and hide away where no one could ever find me.

I tried to be resilient for him. He told me it was shameful that I would react to the pain. That I wasn't strong enough to take his mark. He said I didn't deserve the honor of being an Alpha mate even though it was already done. I wish I'd let him leave me rather than promising to be better. I think, that very first night, I broke a promise with fate by not loving him as a mate should. Even if he had made his claim, I shouldn't have clung to him and promised to be stronger and a worthy mate. I believed the words of the seers and tried to be better for him.

I was a fool.

Because of that, because of me, my family and old pack are dead, all but my niece and nephew, and they aren't far behind. They don't deserve this life. They're so young and innocent. They didn't choose this. I wish I could save them. I wish I could protect them. Most of all, I wish I could go back and not listen to a word from the seers. I should have trusted my instincts, but all the wishes can't take a damn thing back.

For now I protect the pups as best I can. I don't understand why their father keeps me away when he doesn't care about them. Rayne lets them starve, but I'm beaten and chained for trying to give them my food. He won't let them see me. He keeps them away only to hurt them further. Or to hurt me. My body shakes with agony, and my hollow chest tightens in pain. I hate Rayne. My shoulders hunch in anger and defeat as I bring my knees further into my belly. I hate my mate. My lungs heave with a harsh intake of air. I hate this pack.

The spiral haunts me daily as does the guilt of what I've done.

This isn't a strong pack as the seers foretold and as far as ties with his previous pack, he's tried to kill them, tried to cause them pain. I heard what they were planning to do to the pack mates. I'm so thankful they failed. I have no remorse that the members of my own pack are dead. Their hearts have turned black with greed and they delight in harming others. They thrive from one another's resentment and brutality. Tears brim in my eyes as my throat dries, making it difficult to swallow. It got worse and worse, and I couldn't stop it from happening.

There's a sting of pain and then a small push against my belly reminds me of my reason for living. My baby. I let out a hush of a staggered sigh and rub my swollen belly. I close my eyes and imagine a future better than this. My little one apparently has the hiccups, bumping against my pelvic bone with each little jolt of his body. A small, sad laugh escapes me as my whole body warms with the tiniest hint of happiness.

Sleep begs to take me, but with these contractions I know

the time is soon. I pray it is. I have to stay alert, and as soon as I'm given the chance, I'll run. I have to believe it's possible. Without it, without that small scrap of hope, there's no reason to take another breath of this dirty air.

I wish I was stronger. I wish I was faster, but with this extra weight and exhaustion, there's no way I could outrun Shadow's pack. I tried once. Before I was pregnant. Once I realized what kind of wolf Shadow really was. The seers had told me lies, great and horrid lies. Once I opened my eyes and realized what hell I'd been given, I tried to run. It was late and the pack was asleep. I thought if I got a good head start then I could reach my family. I delivered death to my old pack. When he found me just a mile from them, he decided I deserved to be punished. He made me watch, bound and gagged, while his pack crept through the night and murdered every wolf. They hid in the shadows and ambushed my family. I could do nothing to save them. I was as weak then as I am now.

I lay on the cold floor and feel my heavy eyelids fall and brush the threatening tears away. My baby's little hiccups have stopped, and my exhaustion weighs me down. I need to rest, so I give into the need. Another day has gone. I breathe deep, repeating my mantra. Just one day at a time. I can survive just one day at a time.

Just as I feel my body lighten and my breath slow, a large hand wraps around my mouth trapping the scream that rises in my dry throat.

CHAPTER 2

JUDE

The sight of my mate shaking and obviously tormented alone on the cold, hard ground has me grinding my teeth and losing my resolve to not risk everything to destroy every one of them. I have to remind myself over and over again that I'll be back. I'll come back with Devin and the rest of the pack and tear them apart. I'll have Shadow's death once my mate is safe. Every breath he takes is on borrowed time. Another harsh sob shakes her small body, and she grips her belly with both hands as she silently rocks herself. My poor mate.

How could this have happened? My wolf cries in agony inside of me. I've never felt such pain, such a pull to save someone, the need to hold her and heal every pain she's ever had. And yet I have to resist and have to be tactical. I cannot give in to the emotion that overwhelms my very being.

I need to be strong enough to save her, and I pray it's not too late.

With adrenaline rushing into my veins, I take in my surroundings. It didn't take much at all for me to sneak in here. Her hut isn't protected in the least. Like her, it's been abandoned. The anger that sweeps through me forces my knuckles to turn white as I clench my fists. It's fucking freezing so far away from the fire and on the outskirts of the camp. The rest of the pack are tucked away in their own huts, better built and closer to the fire. I have to shut down the desire to slip into each shelter and cut their throats in their sleep. Shadow needs to suffer far more than going peacefully in his sleep. That one thought tempers my anger enough to think clearly and see through the red. This entire pack will suffer for what they've done.

With every step, I'm more and more cautious. I need to get her out of here as quietly and quickly as possible. I'm not sure how to approach her in a way that won't have her screaming. I haven't a clue if she'll fight me or if she can sense me. Inside, my wolf howls again, but there's no response from her. Swallowing thickly, I refuse to think of what that could mean for us. All I know is that the first thing I must do is save her.

The only question is, how?

I can't risk waking the pack. I can't alert them and

compromise my mate's safety. She's on edge as it is, doing her best to hold on to any kind of composure. It's torture to watch. Does this happens often? How many nights has she fallen asleep this way? Alone. Cold. In complete despair.

As the moon dips lower and the darkness is just right, I settle on covering her mouth until she's calm enough to agree to be quiet. Guilt weighs heavily on me, to force her silence by holding her down. With another careful step forward, I hope she feels the pull instantly so she knows I'm her rightful mate. My heart drops with the very real possibility that she won't. Shadow's mark has his essence running through her. I don't know how it will affect our bond. I have to close my eyes to repress the growing snarl in my chest. He'll pay for what he's done.

I breathe deep, calming myself slightly before I walk quietly to my mate. Her shoulders are steady, and her breath has evened somewhat. Her hand continues to gently rub small circles over her belly. I stare at her swollen abdomen, where his child grows, just watching her movements.

His baby.

The thought makes my nostrils flare with rage, but again I calm myself. She shouldn't have to deal with my anger. It's not for her; it's only for him.

For a moment, as she seems to settle and allow sleep to take her, I consider the alternative I'd previously discarded. I thought about leaving her for only a short while to gather the rest of my pack. It would be safer if Devin and the Betas were here to help me. I'd be able to securely get her out of harm's way before destroying this pathetic pack.

But I couldn't bring myself to leave her. I can't stand the fact that she could be hurt if I left her here, even for a few hours. I wouldn't get back until the morning and anything could happen between now and then. I need to get her out of here now. Right fucking now.

Determined it's now or never, I crouch low on the ground behind her. The sound of my jeans moving is barely audible, but it's enough that she stirs slightly. I pause and hold my breath, afraid that any movement or noise is going to wake her. I can't ruin this. I can't have her scream and alert the others. There're far too many in Shadow's pack for me take on alone. If this goes wrong, both my mate and I will most likely die, and it'll be entirely my fault for rushing this. The weight of my decision pushes against my chest and anxiety floods through me.

I remind myself again it's now or never. With my resolve firm, I quickly lean over, cover her mouth, and wrap my hard, muscular arms around her upper body to limit her struggle and try to calm her by shushing into her ear. She immediately tries to scream, but my hand muffles her cries.

Fuck! Heat engulfs me as she struggles against me, and I have to keep her still without hurting her. Her strangled cry was loud enough that my wolf goes on high alert. His hackles raise. Her body lifts off the floor and bucks against me with a force I wasn't expecting.

My mate still has fight in her. Even with my hand over her mouth, she tries again to scream, and she pushes against me with all her weight. I lay heavily against her, but my eyes are firmly focused on her belly. I can't put my full weight on her or push against her with the force needed to keep her still. The sounds of her struggling against me and trying to scream are resonating through the small hut, and if any of the shifters are awake, I'm certain they'll hear her.

My heart rampages as I shush her.

"Shh!" I push my bicep against her chest and firmly grab her small throat in my hand while whispering into her ear, "Quiet." I don't want my hold on her to be threatening, but I know it is. At my voice, she goes still and stops fighting my hold on her. With every hard thump, I can feel her heart race and her body heat with worry. My wolf whines in my chest, wanting to ensure his mate is all right. There's no response from her or her wolf though. Only silence.

After a long moment, with her still and her eyes wide open, I slowly release my grip on her throat, and the move allows her body to relax slightly into mine. I fucking love it. I love the feel of her body against mine.

For a moment I think our bond must be calming her, hope blooms and I dare to feel relief. I loosen my hand on her mouth and the second I do, my mate, my feisty little mate, bites down on my middle finger without any restraint. Fuck! I struggle to contain the scream climbing up my throat. Her teeth sink in deeper and deeper, breaking through the skin. The rest of her body remains still with the exception of her eyes narrowing in the dark.

I twist my body slightly and curl my toes in an effort to mute my pain. My other hand grips her hip before loosening and stroking gently down her side, fighting the instinct to pry her mouth open. Through gritted teeth, I command her as quietly as possible with only the hint of my pain showing, "Let go." I speak in monosyllables because that's all I can manage. "You're safe." Her body stiffens and there's a slight change in her demeanor. Her mouth hesitantly opens, and I yank my finger away. Trace amounts of my blood lingering on her pale lips are barely visible in the faint moonlight. Even with my eyes adjusted to the dark, I can only make out faint details of my mate.

My mate. A mate who can't feel the pull I do. A mate who has no idea I've come to save her. As the seconds pass and she eyes me warily, it's all too obvious. She doesn't recognize me as her mate. I slowly move away from her, but she remains still, and I know it's because she doesn't trust me. She's waiting for my next move.

I hover over her body so she can see me, and I offer her my hand—not the one she fucking bit. "I'm going to get you out of here." I attempt to reassure her. "Take my hand." At first, she merely glances at my hand and then glances at the opening to the hut. I almost beg her, the plea is on my lips, but then she moves.

She places her small palm in mine but doesn't grip my hand at all. Her hesitation makes my wolf howl in agony. "Come." I give the simple low command and pull her closer to the entry, but she doesn't budge. Her feet stay planted on the dirt and her other hand holds the tattered blanket closer to her, shielding herself from me. I glance behind me when another firm tug from my hand doesn't get her moving. Her eyes are wide and full of fear as she starts frantically shaking her head.

A low growl forms in my throat. She has to come with me. She better come with me. She's my mate. Not his! My gut churns in pain. There's no way she could possibly want to stay, not with the way they treat her. As I devised escape plans while waiting on the pack to sleep, I didn't envision her resistance to leave. At least not after she realized I wasn't a threat. I swallow the lump in my throat and move to fully face her. I part my lips in a last-ditch effort to convince her before I forcibly remove her from this shithole.

Before I can speak she barely whispers, "My niece and nephew, Addison and Reece." I stare blankly at her, waiting for more. "I can't leave without them." Her wide eyes plead with me as they turn glassy with tears.

Then realization dawns on me. The pups. I nod in

understanding. "Be quiet." I stop just before leaving the hut, before I become visible, and I hesitate, thinking maybe I should leave her here while I grab the children. Just in case someone wakes. But if something happens, I need her by my side. I need to make sure she's protected. Uneasiness rips through me.

I don't fucking like this. It's too dangerous. There's too much at risk. I grasp her hand tighter and pull her closer before taking the nape of her neck in my other hand and lowering my face to hers. "Stay close." Her beautiful hazel eyes search mine for a short moment before she nods. Our lips are so close; I desperately want to kiss her. Does she feel it now?

I want nothing more than to take her as my own. She pulls away from me before I even have a chance. My heart clenches as she stares back at me with concern and uncertainty. There aren't any signs that she feels the pull to me, and that fucking kills both me and my wolf.

I have to remind myself that fate can be a cruel bitch, but she always has her reasons.

She brushes her arm against my back as I push my body in front of hers at the entry to the hut. It faces the rest of camp, so we would easily be seen if anyone wakes and glances outside. The night will cloak us far better in the woods. I grip her small hand in mine, not willing to let go. My jaw ticks as I slowly walk into the dark night, keeping her behind me.

With every step closer into camp, rather than away, my heart pounds. I stalk slowly toward the edge of camp near the trees. My car's parked nearly a mile away, through the forest. It's going to be hard enough getting her through the trees without making too much noise, let alone her and two pups. I peer back, debating on stealing her away, but when her eyes catch mine, I know she will never leave them.

I'm certain I saw the pups go into a hut on the other side of this shitty camp site. They went in with a large wolf, so I know they won't be alone. I start to weigh the risk in my head and then curse myself for even considering not taking them.

Once we get to the edge of the forest line, I pause and turn, quickly lifting my mate in my arms. She stills at my touch but allows me to carry her with her arms wrapped around my neck to steady herself. Her fear is evident in her darting eyes and short breaths. I do my best not to jostle her. I don't want to cause her or her pup any pain. Jealousy and anger creep up at the thought of her carrying Shadow's child, but I push it down.

I take a few steady steps away from camp into the dark cover of the forest, but she pushes away from my body, almost causing me to drop her. Her small noises are enough that she could potentially alert the pack. I grip her tighter and let a small, low growl escape my throat in anger at her efforts to leave me.

She stares straight into my angered gaze and speaks in

a firm, yet low, voice. "I won't leave them." Her bravery is admirable, but I wish she'd just trust me.

"You will stay where I leave you and I will get them." There is no compromise in my demand. I'm not taking her back there. No fucking way.

"They won't go with you. They'll scream." Although her voice is soft and full of apprehension, her expression is one of determination. As the precious seconds slip by, I consider her words and I have to admit that she's right. I'll have to handle them as I did her. But there are two of them and a wolf that could easily wake if they scream before I cover their mouths.

Once again, I'm reminded of how dangerous this task is.

Knowing all too well the consequences of failing, I move quickly, holding her tight to me as I walk through the forest, staying out of sight, gaining ground toward the pups. I carefully step through the brush with slow, deliberate steps. The branches bend under my weight and I shift slightly to avoid breaking them. There's nothing I can do about the dried leaves and debris, though. I move as slowly as possible, hoping the sounds of the night cover the low crunching beneath my feet. It takes far too long for my comfort, but there isn't any movement in the camp, so I try to ignore the time ticking by. I can do this slowly, the night is long.

My heart pumps louder, racing in my ears, as we near their hut. If only I could simply turn around and take my mate away from here with a clear conscious, I would. But I can't leave the pups and it's obvious that she'll fight me if I even think about trying. At least their hut is closest to the trees—that's the only gift I've been granted in this shitty situation. We'll grab them quickly and quietly before heading into the forest and straight for my car. The pack will lose our tracks there and we'll be safe. Although I'll be returning to give Shadow what he truly deserves.

I walk with her in my arms, and her tiny fist clutches my shirt as we move into the clearing, away from our cover and closer to danger. I gently set her down, but keep her body pinned to mine. Her swollen belly hits my chest as I stand, and again I'm reminded of the fact that she's carrying Shadow's child. Her bare feet gain purchase in the grass, but I keep my hands firm on her wide hips. My blunt fingernails dig into her skin; I just can't let go. A bad feeling grows in my gut, and I feel as if I stop holding her, even for just a moment, I'll never be able to hold her again.

My blood rushes cold through my veins, chilling every inch of my body. Terror grips me; I don't want to let her go. She looks up through her thick lashes and her gaze pierces into me. Her hazel eyes are mesmerizing as they plead with me to give her this. It calms my wolf like I've never felt. She already holds a power over me that I can't explain. I know she needs this. She needs them.

I grit my teeth and slowly release my firm grip. I'm not sure how I should stand as we move from the safety of the trees. The closer we get to the pups, every angle will present a danger to her. I can't stand the thought that I won't be able to shield her from harm's way.

I decide to enter the hut first; if that fucker's awake I'll rip his throat out without hesitation. I won't give him the chance to scream. I hate that I'm risking the safety of my mate. With one step in, I leave my arm out with my hand firmly clamped on hers. It takes a moment for my eyes to adjust now that I no longer have the light of the moon to lead my way. I settle my eyes on a large form in the center of the hut. The prick is sleeping on his stomach, his shoulders rising slowly and steadily. I wait a minute to make sure he's really asleep before searching the remainder of the small area. I recognize the fucker to be the one who grabbed my mate by her hair, and I resist the urge to just slit his throat. The only thing keeping me from doing it is the fact that the pups are in the room. They don't deserve to see that.

My nose scrunches as I take in the smell of whiskey and urine. Sure enough, empty glass bottles litter the floor. I make a note to be cautious while making my way to the pups. Behind the man are two small bodies, both curled and wrapped around each other, obviously cold. My gaze heats with anger as I notice the only blanket in the room is covering the man who's sleeping soundly. I'm nearly overwhelmed with the need to rip it from his body and wake the bastard just to beat the shit out of him. I close my eyes for only a moment, putting my emotions in check.

Waving my head ever so slightly, I motion for my mate to enter. She moves with quiet, deliberate steps. The sight of the man doesn't cause her to stop; she moves past him with agility, even though the weight of her belly seems to make her body tilt forward with each step. Her legs are shaky and her balance is slightly off. It makes me want to reach out to her and help her, but there's no fucking way I'm taking my eyes off this massive shifter who's only a foot away from my mate. I'm focused on him while she's focused on getting the pups.

I glance quickly at my stealthy mate. She's squatting next to the pups' sleeping forms and gently places her soft hand on the little girl. The pup shifts in her sleep and the sound of her slight movements makes my eyes dart back to the fucker I should probably just kill. With bated breath, I watch my mate stroke the backs of each of the children, trying to wake them gently.

They're so small, I wonder how old they are. They can't be much older than a year or two; their movements earlier were so clumsy. In my old pack, before Devin, there were plenty of little ones, but I hardly paid them any attention. The women cared for them. My father had three pups, all boys. I was the oldest, my twin brothers were only a year younger than me. So I've never bothered myself with small children, I've never had to. But here I am in a room about to rescue two children, with a mate who's pregnant.

Fuck, life can really throw you a curve ball.

The little girl's eyes open slowly as she turns to lay on her back and look up at my mate. She's a bit bigger than the boy, so I imagine she's older. A small smile slips into place, but as my mate places her finger over her lips and releases a small, "shh," the little girl's eyes dart to her father and then to me. Her eyes widen and she pales instantly. It's a look of fear. My mate places her small hand on the girl's cheek and tilts her head to face her. She mouths the words "it's okay." Fortunately, the girl is easily swayed by my mate, and I let out a heavy breath. My mate motions for the little girl to stand and hold onto her and she obliges, looking back at the other pup and giving my mate a questioning and worried look. She nods her head before handing the little girl to me.

I've never held a child, but I reach across the shifter's sleeping body and take the little girl in my arms. My mate doesn't waste any time reaching for the next pup. The little girl eyes me warily and I do my best to avoid her gaze, focusing instead of my mate. She gently picks up the sleeping little boy and tries to turn, but her balance is fucking awful and she nearly falls. She's quick to steady herself, but the sudden jolt to the little boy wakes him. As the child looks up at my mate, a huge smile brightens his sleepy face, but then he opens his mouth. My mate raises the hand she's steadying herself with to her lips, but it's too late.

"Lulu!" The little pup's squeal has my eyes darting to the

sleeping shifter. Angry silver eyes stare back at me. Fuck! A loud growl echoes off the mud walls as I drop the little girl. Before he has a chance to rise, I grab his throat in my hand and push the strong shifter back down onto the bed. The little girl whimpers as my mate grabs both pups and runs out of the hut, an arm around each of their tiny waists, balancing them on her hips. I hear movement and rough, tired voices from the camp as my palm pushes against the shifters mouth to keep him quiet.

I grip his throat tighter as he thrashes under me. My knees keep his arms pinned as he struggles to gain freedom and attempts to suck in air. Every ounce of anger and fear I've felt for hours tightens my grip. His body bucks against mine but I keep him pinned, having the obvious advantage. Adrenaline races through me, I push down with all my might, covering his mouth to muffle the noises and crushing his windpipe. I can't let him live. I can't risk the pack coming after us so soon. My heart pounds with the thought of my mate and those pups, unprotected, running through the forest. I listen for the sounds of the other shifters, but the night is quiet as I continue to push all of my weight onto this asshole.

Whoever woke up from the initial noise isn't making a sound at the moment. I pray they go back to sleep and don't look around. The shifter's milky eyes spike with red as his face puffs and sweats. I watch him as my knuckles around his throat turn white. Looking into his hard eyes, they slowly turn red as the blood vessels break, and I choke him to death.

The second his body goes limp, I'm off him and following the scent of my mate through the camp and to the edge of the forest. My heart races, keeping me on high alert. I can easily hear them running frantically through the trees, just as easily as I hear the sounds of the shifters slowly waking up. My mate and the pups are making too much noise. It's only a matter of time before curiosity turns to alarm and the wolves realize what's happening. I bolt through the forest, crushing branches and brushing my large body against the bark. It scrapes my skin, but with all the adrenaline pumping through me, I don't feel a damn thing. Being quiet is no longer an option. I need speed. I need to get to them and get to my car as soon as possible.

They are literally running for their lives.

Through the darkness, I barely spot my mate as soon as I enter the tree line. She's struggling to hold both pups and run. The sight of her cradling a child on each hip as she scrambles through the brush is terrifying. She wouldn't get far on her own, I've already nearly caught up to her. As soon as I reach my mate, I hear the pack behind me. A loud howl is followed quickly with barks and growls of fury. Fuck, they found him.

They're coming for us.

"This way." I speak so my mate knows it's me that's coming up behind her, but she still let's out a small scream as I reach for her and grab her. As if it couldn't get any worse, the growl of knowing snarls echoes behind us.

"Hold onto them." I hold her as tight as I can without squishing the now crying pups or her belly. It's a fucking challenge. The bulkiness of all of us makes running through the trees much harder than it should be. My muscles scream as I push them faster and harder than I ever have. The quickest way back to my car leads us through a section of forest where the trees are far too close together for me to fit all of us at once. I have to scatter my approach and shuffle us around the trees, ducking through branches and jumping over fallen trunks. My arm scrapes against the bark, but I push forward. Better my arm than the pups. My lungs heave for air, but I push forward. I recognize the path I took earlier and feel slight relief that we're close.

That reprieve doesn't last as I hear the sound of several shifters barreling toward us through the forest. They must be in wolf form to be running so fast. Fuck, I wish I could hold onto my mate and the pups in wolf form. We would already be there. But we're close. The pup on my mate's left hip screams, no doubt realizing that we're being chased. I push faster as a cold sweat breaks along my skin and my muscles ache.

Just as I see my car in the clearing ahead, a pup slips. I grab the little girl by the nape and keep running while struggling to keep my mate on my hip. I can't hold onto them for much longer, but I can see the car and my mate is gripping onto me with everything she has. I nearly crash my body into the steel frame, only slowing the tiniest bit to save me from crushing my mate and the pups. I yank the passenger door open and push them in before climbing across the front of my car to get to the driver's door. I shove the key in the ignition while the pups climb over the console and my mate furiously tries to get them in the back safely.

Their door is still open as I reverse through the small clearing and see the wolves sprinting toward us. My arm steadies my mate as I slam on the gas pedal. I fishtail the car, making the door swing open even farther and slam the pedal to the floor. My mate and the young pups scream from the sudden movement, but they hold on. The tires spin in the dirt before jolting forward, pushing our backs into the seats and slamming the door closed. They're fast, but not fast enough. I don't let up on the gas until I see the wolves halt, four in a line, howling and snarling in anger, and watching our car grow smaller as I increase the distance between us.

CHAPTER 3

LENA

The massive shifter glances at me what seems like every five seconds. He keeps lifting his hands off the wheel as though he's going to touch me too, but to my relief, he doesn't. There's a thick tension, a heat I can't describe, but fear is what outweighs everything.

What have I done? If Shadow finds us...we're dead.

The silence has stretched the entire drive, apart from me reassuring the pups that everything was fine and to sleep. I glance in the back seat, continuing to ignore the shifter who helped us, and watch my niece and nephew breathe easily in their sleep.

After an hour and a half of driving, I've only just now given up the fear that they're following us. I kept looking back with a sick tension in the pit of my stomach and the instinct still hasn't quite left me. The lump in my throat hasn't diminished in the least, and I can't stop thinking about what Shadow would do to me if he caught me this time. I swallow in an attempt to breathe and look back to Addy and Reece again; they're still huddled together in the back under a blanket. Peacefully sleeping I hope. I'm far too aware nightmares could follow them, but I pray they don't.

The smells of dirt and blood fill the car, but more than that is the fear that radiates from the pups. My heart aches at the memory of their terror-filled eyes. My poor niece and nephew. I want to climb into the back with them, but they sleep easier together just the two of them, so there's no room to lay...that and I feel frozen in my seat with this stranger's sharp silver eyes on me.

I don't understand. I don't know what to think. A small part of me is relieved to be away from Shadow, but the rest of me is terrified of the unknown. I have no clue what's going on and it's hard to be grateful when I know a worse fate could be waiting for me.

"Who are you?" I dare to ask, the questions and thoughts scream in my head, demanding answers. My whispered question finally breaks the silence.

I don't remember him from my old pack; I have no memory of him at all. My eyes fall as I realize he couldn't have come from my pack; they're all dead. The lump grows thicker in my dry throat, and I struggle to take a breath of air.

I need to keep myself together for the pups' sake, but I start to tremble as I realize I've given this shifter control by getting in this car with him. I'm at his mercy and I have no idea why he's come for me. I'm reminded of my vulnerability as the pup growing inside of me kicks against my ribs. I close my eyes and wince as I absorb the painful blow. My little wolf. As the pinching pain subsides, the hint of relief comes over me. He's okay. My baby is okay. We've survived this long, we can make it another day. My hand finds my belly and I close my eyes for a brief moment of calm. Just one day at a time.

The werewolf's large hands twist on the wheel and the movement and sound have my eyes darting to him once again. He looks at me from the corner of his eye again.

"Jude." His low, baritone voice sends a shot of heat through me, and an unwarranted desire heats my core. My heart sputters in my chest. I have no clue where that came from; I have no right to be feeling this way toward him. He's a beast of a man, taking up space with his broad shoulders. His chiseled jaw looks rough with its stubble.

As I find myself eyeing him, my breathing shallows and I clear my throat while I readjust in my seat. It protests my movement with a groan and instinctively I look back to check on the children. The movement is accompanied with another pang of pain. One that is short lived but other pains shine through. My lower back is killing me and I can't get comfortable. Not that being uncomfortable is unusual at this point in my pregnancy.

Jude pushes a button on the dash of his car. "Give it a minute to heat the seat"—his eyes find mine—"it'll help with the pain."

His voice is full of concern. It's kind of him to care, but he's already done enough.

Something about his tenor makes me feel at ease, like it's going to be all right. As the seat warms, he's right, it eases the pain. I'm slow to relax, but then I find myself staring at the side of his gorgeous face. He's handsome yet rugged. There's mud on the scruff of his five o'clock shadow, traveling up to his high cheek bones; he's classically handsome with his short, dark hair and piercing silver eyes. He turns to look at me and I shift in my seat to stare out of the window and avoid his questioning gaze.

As the heat slowly warms my back, I feel a radiating ache travel from my lower back down to the front of my thighs. I push both my palms against my legs to alleviate the pain while my eyes close tightly and my toes curl. I hold in my whimper and breathe out deeply. It's not that bad of a pain and it's not the first time I've felt it. I've learned to be as quiet as I can. They've been coming and going this past week. As the pain subsides, I relax back into the seat. Jude's watching me instead of the road, which makes me uneasy.

"I'm fine." I push the words out as the uncomfortable sensation wanes.

"You're not." His words are low and absolute.

"I am. They're just Braxton Hicks. They're fake contractions." I lower my gaze to my scraped knees which have mostly healed. "I promise it's nothing more." I don't think he would go through all this trouble to kick me out of his car if I were to go into labor, but I don't want to risk it. I'm getting close to the end of my pregnancy, but it's been hard tracking the weeks. The lonely days have blurred together and I'm not even sure at which point I came to carry Shadow's young.

I feel the blood drain from my face as the overwhelming sadness washes over me. Just the thought of my mate makes my heart clench in agony. I don't feel any regret that I've left him; I just feel weak and dejected that I'll forever be alone. Every memory is dark and brutal. I rub my belly, feeling a bit of peace, at least I have my pup. I'll do everything I can to do right by him.

"We're almost home." Jude's words bring me back to reality. Home? I glance in the back of the car to see both pups are still soundly asleep.

"Where are you taking us?" My voice is weak and breaks at the end of the question. The anxiety I felt when we first got in the car has returned.

"Home." His simple answer doesn't ease my worry. Anxiousness riddles its way through me. He gently places his large hand on my thigh and my body stills from his touch. I close my eyes just as another radiating wave of pain begins in my lower back. I breathe deep, but this time I don't move my hand to my upper thighs since his hand would be in my way. I dig my heels into the floor of the car and breathe through the uncomfortable pain. Once it's gone, I realize he's taken his hand away from me and is gripping the wheel with a force that's turned his knuckles white.

"What do you mean 'home'?" I have to push through these questions and figure out what I've gotten us into. I let out a slow, shaky breath before asking, "Are we staying with your pack?"

"Yes." His one-word answer doesn't ease my worries in the least.

He looks out of the window while I stare at my dirty feet on the floor. I just can't look at him without feeling nauseated. My chest hurts and I rub the growing knot of pain.

I nod my head and swallow before asking, "Whose pack is it? Who sent you?"

"The Shadow Falls pack." My body freezes with fear. I know that name. It's Shadow's old pack. Tears prick my eyes as I realize why I've been taken. Shadow wanted to hurt their pack, and tried to take their mates, so Devin sent someone after me.

I close my eyes tight to avoid crying, but the pain comes back. I wish it would stop; I have more important things to concern myself with now. I need to know what they plan to do.

with me and my family. My hands push against my thighs and my shoulders hunch forward. I try to relax my body to loosen the pain, but in this position it's so hard to get comfortable.

"We're almost there." His words are meant to be reassuring based on his tone, but all they do is terrify me. I've been taken by my mate's enemy, and I have no clue how I'm going to get out of this. My mantra rings in my head, one day at a time, but I don't want to think like that. Not when Addy and Reece are involved.

"What are you going to do to us?" My breath stalls as I ask; I need to know. I need to know they'll be all right no matter what plans they have for me.

His silver eyes finally meet mine, but I can't keep his gaze. I'm terrified that they're going to use us against Shadow, or worse, send us back. I hear him swallow before answering, "I'm keeping you. You belong to me."

A numbing heat washes over me as fear settles in my bones.

I've merely changed hands of captors.

With staggered breathing, I attempt to remain calm. I nod stiffly, acknowledging his words, as tears slip down my cheeks.

"What about Addy and Reece?" I swallow thickly, praying that he'll show me kindness.

"They'll stay with us." He turns the wheel and immediately the car starts rocking unsteadily as we drive down a gravel road. I close my eyes and try to even my breathing. As long as my family is safe, we'll get through this. I don't have any other choice but to do my best to survive. I will survive.

Before I've had a moment to really pull myself together, the car slows and comes to a stop. I open my eyes to see an enormous house in front of us. The driveway is a semicircle that leads to a stone path and large entry. I've never seen such a beautiful home. Jude's hand grabs mine and he squeezes. "I promise you'll be all right. I'll take care of you." His voice is soft and comforting and I find myself believing him, but then a flash of Shadow comes to the forefront of my mind. My body stiffens. He said the same words. He said he'd take care of me. I look back up at the house and it no longer holds its appeal. It's merely a gilded cage. I won't let myself be conned with fantasies. Not again. I won't let it happen again.

I lower my head in shame for hoping for more than what this reality is. I've been taken by the enemy of my mate and given to one of his pack members. I look into Jude's silver gaze and bite the inside of my cheek, thinking maybe he'll treat me better.

But why would he? Just as the thought strikes me another wave of pain grows in my back and moves slowly to my front and down my thighs.

"I'll get the pups, we have plenty of room."

Before I can answer, Jude's already gotten up and out of his seat and shut the car door. He moves to the back seat to get the pups and I know I should do the same. I move through the pain, breathing slow deliberate breaths out of my mouth in through my nose as I open the door and scramble out. I lean against the back of the car as I hear him shut the opposite door. With the soft click of the door closing, I look up to see him carrying both sleeping pups. Part of me is relieved that I won't have to carry them, I'm exhausted and just want to rest; but the other part of me is ashamed that I can't take care of my only remaining family.

I watch him as he makes his way around the car with Addison sleeping on his right shoulder, open mouthed and drooling; and Reece asleep on his left, reminiscent of a peaceful little angel. I'm all too aware that I shouldn't feel this sense of calm without knowing what's to come. It's short lived anyway; the air is knocked out of me as my little pup kicks me again. I grunt and close my eyes. My strong little wolf.

"Do you need a healer?" I open my eyes slowly to see an enormous, muscular wolf in front of me. His face is all sharp edges, and waves of dominance and power wash off him. The Alpha, Devin. I feel an urge to bow to him, but his hand reaches out and braces my elbow. "You don't look well." His voice is strong and emotionless. He's merely stating a fact.

Anxiousness creeps through me.

"Yes, she needs a healer." Jude answers for me and I hunch my shoulders forward realizing I'm not needed to speak. I nod my head slightly and walk with the men up the steps to the house.

"Do you think they'll follow you here?" Devin speaks over

me to Jude.

"It would be easier, but I don't think they will. We'll have to go to them." I part my lips in shock as the air leaves my lungs. They're going after Shadow's pack.

The echoes of our footsteps are hollow as the beautifully carved front door opens and we enter the estate.

"They're here!" A feminine squeal draws my eyes across the spacious entry to a large and modern kitchen. My jaw nearly drops at the luxury. It's been years since I've even seen a kitchen, and it wasn't even close to being this nice.

"Hush, the children are sleeping." Hearing those words from the Alpha is odd, but even more strange is watching a small human walk past him and straight to me. I almost back away, but she wraps her arms around me. She smells wonderful and I immediately feel sickened at my appearance in comparison, but she doesn't seem to notice. If she does, she doesn't let on.

A human and a wolf, the connection between them is as obvious as it is confusing. She cannot be the Alpha mate, can she?

The dirt from my clothing clings to the human's clothes when she releases me. "Welcome to the pack." A bright smile lights her face as she whispers in a hushed tone.

"Aw look at them sleeping." A low, sing-song voice whispers from a tall blonde to my right, another human. I should be grateful that the confusion and shock replace the uncertainty and fear. She places a hand over her heart and a small smile grows on her face as she watches Jude carry Addy and Reece into a room opposite the kitchen. I instantly follow, my heart racing and my head filled with questions. I need to know exactly where he's taking them. I'm grateful for their kindness, but I don't trust it.

He lays them down so gently on the sofa, carefully so they remain asleep. I can barely breathe watching the Alpha rest a blanket over them before looking back at Jude, not saying a word out loud, but it's more than obvious they're speaking through the bond.

"We're converting the guest wing for the kids." The blonde whispers and I'm not quite sure who she's talking to.

"Yeah we don't need it. I just cleared out the last of my things." I barely hear the brunette talk behind me as I watch Jude take a step back and give the pups space to sleep. His eyes peer into mine as he murmurs "they'll be all right" and motions for us to back slowly away. Cautiously, I do. I follow them.

"We have so much to buy for them. If you'd called us, we would've had everything ready." Jude huffs at the blonde's joking admonishment. It dawns on me that they must've been talking through their pack bond while we were driving. "The guys are gonna watch the pups until we get back. Do you want anything in particular or can I have free rein to shop?" It takes me a moment to realize the question was directed at me. The perky blonde stares at me expectantly. I can't help my blank stare. I don't know what I expected, but this wasn't it. I'm so out of my element and I don't know what's expected of me. I'm afraid if I say the wrong thing, I'll be punished.

Jude's hands brace my shoulders as he once again speaks over me. "Buy everything they need. Just don't take too long."

"Thirty minutes, tops." She retorts, and her smile dims slightly as she looks back at me but she's quick to correct it. I can only imagine what they're saying through their bond.

My eyes focus on the floor as another round of pain settles in my lower back and works its way to my front. I have to close my eyes and suppress the low moan clawing at me to get out. They continue to talk, and I do my best to stay out of the way and stay quiet. I try my damndest to just get through this pain without alerting them.

I don't know what to say. I'm grateful for their warm welcome, but I don't understand it and my instinct is to leave. I open my mouth, but words fail to escape my dry throat. I suddenly feel cold, and I wrap my arms around my shoulders. I focus on the floor again, unsure of myself and what I should be doing.

"Would you like a shower, Lulu?" Hearing my nephew's nickname for me from the handsome, masculine shifter forces a small, sad pang of a laugh from my lips.

After a moment I'm able to answer, "Lena."

"Lena." There's a hint of awe in Jude's voice and it commands me to look into his silver eyes. They're soft and they call to me. Small wrinkles form around his eyes to make him look even more attractive. My body wants me to lean into his embrace, but I refrain from giving into the temptation. I'm tired and aching everywhere.

"Would you like a shower, Lena? We have clothes for you."

Tears prick at the kindness, and I realize I may have thought the worst. I would give anything for a shower.

"Please." I finally answer his question. He looks back at me with a mix of uncertainty and hopefulness.

"Please what?"

"The shower." My voice is small as I tear my gaze away from his.

"This way." His strong hand presses against the small of my back just as another false contraction rips through me. It's more than irritating at this point. I walk through the pain and do my best not to let it get to me. I need to keep a level head and not get distracted. Jude rubs his hand along my back, and I find it relaxing and comforting. So much so that my eyes start to drift. I follow the sound of his shoes hitting the floor and let him lead me.

"Are you sure you wouldn't rather have a bath?" His question makes me open my eyes and look up at him. A comforting smile plays at his lips, but concern is most evident on his handsome face.

I shake my head. I'm covered in filth. The river has been too cold for me to wash lately. I really need to clean myself.

Of everything. "A shower please." I can't help that my words come out as though I'm begging. Quite frankly, I would beg if he asked me to or rather, if he demanded.

I don't get the sense that he'll be doing much asking. The thought sends a chill through my body. It's been so long since I've even seen a shower. I'd give anything to be bathed in hot water. My head rocks as a wave of dizziness washes over me. At the same time another bout of pain nearly collapses my body. This one is much stronger than the last few. I have to stop and lean against the wall. Jude keeps his hands on me, and I find myself pushing him away. The pain in my legs makes me crouch forward to put pressure against my thighs. It feels so much better with the pressure from my hands, but my back still fucking hurts.

Jude waits patiently, gently rubbing my back even though I pushed him away. If he's going to have his hands on me I wish he'd push harder. I need pressure to ease this pain. I can't open my mouth to speak though, instead I just concentrate on breathing. For the first time I wonder if this is it, but my water hasn't broken, so I doubt I'm truly in labor. I breathe through my nose as the contraction wanes, and I gain control of my composure again.

"Are you sure you're all right?" I hear Jude's strong voice and simply nod in response. I walk forward with my eyes mostly closed. I just need a shower and a nap. That's all. Then I'll feel better.

"I know there's a lot you need, but anything at this moment? Is there anything I can do?"

It's shocking to hear his softly worded question. There's a tension between us as I stare up into his gaze and I gently shake my head.

I nearly weep as he leads me into the room. His bathroom is larger than my pathetic hut back at camp. The walls and floor are made of large rectangular slats of white marble with gray streaks. There's a large, egg-shaped bath in the center of the room and the entire back wall is a walk-in shower with three shower heads, one in the ceiling and the two on either side of the stall. A large pane of glass makes up the door. It's gorgeous and so clean it's nearly sterile. The sight makes me feel so out of place. It emphasizes my insignificance and filth.

If this is all a trick, it's cruel.

"I don't feel comfortable leaving you." Jude's voice sounds odd. He sounds unsure for the first time. I turn to face him with my arms wrapped around my body. I swallow before looking into his eyes. He's asking me for permission, sort of. At least it seems as though his eyes are asking for my permission for him to stay. I nod my head slightly.

"Could you just stay outside the door?" He's made it clear that he intends to keep me, though I'm not quite sure why yet or what he plans to do with me, but I can only imagine one reason.

"I'd rather not. You don't seem stable." His voice is soft

and low, nearly apologetic. "I could stare at the wall, if you'd rather. But I'd like to see you and make sure you're well."

His cadence and carefully chosen words leave me at his mercy.

I nod and slowly start to peel off the dirty clothes from my body. My fingers drift over my bare, swollen stomach. I can feel the little indents from the stretch marks on the lower half of my belly. I haven't thought much of them since they appeared. It's not as though anyone was going to see them. I look down and see that I now have several marks along the outside of my breasts also. They've swollen recently, but I hadn't realized they'd give me stretch marks as well. I put my insecurities behind me and drop the clothes in a dirty pile on the clean, white floor and walk forward with purpose. I keep my head down and avoid eye contact with Jude. I can hear him walking behind me, but he's at least giving me some distance.

I have to uncross my arms to open the door to the shower, but I hesitate. I don't like him watching me. It feels so wrong. If he senses my uneasiness, he doesn't show it. His large frame closes in on me as I step into the shower. I turn to stare at him; he's fully clothed, yet he doesn't stop outside of the stall. He reaches past me, making me take a small step back closer to the tiled wall as my hands grip my shoulders, allowing my forearms to cover my breasts. I watch as he turns the dials for the shower head and a spray of water comes down behind me, just missing my body. I back against the other side of the stall while he gauges the temperature of the water. I don't need him to do this, and the act itself is filling my head with more and more questions. I wish he would just leave me be, but I'm in no position to ask for anything. I should be grateful and ensure he has no reason to be upset with me.

After another short moment, I get my wish.

"I'll wait outside. I'll be listening though, so if you need anything, don't hesitate."

I don't reach his eyes even though I can feel his gaze on me. I only nod and whisper, "Thank you."

Perhaps it's the pain, perhaps it's gratitude...maybe it's the fear. I don't know why I don't feel more violated. It could be the sheer exhaustion.

As I hear the door close, my entire body feels heavier and sags. My legs are weak as I walk slowly into the spray of hot water and rest my forehead against the cold wall. I try to relax my shoulders under the spray, but my body seems to ache more and more as the time passes. The warmth is welcoming, but it's not enough to settle this uneasiness running through me. I stay there, under the spray, for a long time, just wishing the pain would go away. All of the pain.

I hesitantly reach for the bottle of soap sitting on the corner shelf. It's not mine. None of this is mine. I think he intended for me to use it, but I still hesitate. I feel so unsure and unsteady. I stand under the flowing streams staring at the bottle but decide not to use it. I don't want to make him or anyone else angry. He's been kind so far; I don't want to give him a reason to be upset. The water will be enough. I run my fingers through my hair to try to untangle the knots. I struggle for a few moments and then decide to just let the water run through it more before I try again.

I rub my belly as I feel the pressure of another contraction growing in my lower back. I lean forward and put my hands where I need them on my upper thighs and breathe through the pain. A low moan vibrates through my body as I sway with the contraction. The deep moan makes the pain seem somewhat bearable. I feel hot and exhausted, and I wish it would just stop. If only these contractions would let up for a little while. I just need a break so I can rest.

I don't even realize Jude's come into the bathroom until his voice is right behind me.

CHAPTER 4

JUDE

The second I hear that moan of pain from her lips I burst through the door. Against every logical thought, I'm led to her and I can't stop myself. It fucking killed me to leave, but it hurt even more watching her dejected and uncomfortable in my presence. It's as if merely being in the same room as me was painful for her.

With my heart racing, assuming the worst from her groan of pain, I don't hesitate to open the shower door. The steam blinds me for a moment and then I see she's hunched over and pushing her hands against her thighs. She looks as if she's dying. She's not fucking okay.

"Where's the healer?" I shout in my head at Devin as my

heart pounds even harder.

"I won't let her die. I can't allow this. She needs help and she needs it now." This can't be normal. Fuck! I just found my mate and here she is doubled over in pain. Even through her small moans of protest, I pick her up easily, careful not to jostle her too much, and bring her to the bed. She may be on death's door, but she has enough fight in her to scramble away from my hold.

"I'm just bringing you to the bed," I reassure her as she bears down with pain again.

"She's coming." Devin answers in my head and I just shake my head at his response, watching Lena get on her knees in the middle of the bed and moan into the sheets.

"What the fuck do I do?" My voice is weak as shit, but I'm so far out of my element I don't care. This pain in my chest is unbearable. Even my wolf howls in agony.

"Hold on." Devin doesn't seem bothered, and I don't fucking like it.

"I'm watching my mate die, Devin." I barely get out the words. The fear and helplessness are numbing.

"Lena," I murmur her name as I approach, but she doesn't respond more than a groan that rocks with her body.

"You want me to come in there and see your mate like that, Jude?" I snarl at Devin's question and it makes Lena whimper. My hands run down my face.

"Give it a minute. Grace knew a doula."

"What the fuck is a doula?"

Not more than a minute later the door opens, and I watch Lizzie and Grace quietly enter my bedroom, each with a MacBook in hand. Grace is more skittish than Lizzie, who approaches Lena without showing an ounce of anything other than compassion.

Grace, dressed like Lizzie in pajamas, glances at me and then whispers that Lena's okay. "This is just childbirth."

Blood drains from my face at her statement. There is no fucking way this is normal.

"Lena sweetie, how would you rate your pain on a scale from one to ten?" Lizzie asks as she sets the computer down on the bed and walks quickly to Lena's side. Grace grabs a chair from the corner of the room and drags it over to the bed. All I can do is watch.

Lena lifts her head up to look at the two of them. "A seven. I'd say it's a seven." Her answer shocks me. Just a seven?

"What medicine can she have to take the pain away?" I ask them. "What do we have?" I try to think of what kind of pills we have in the house, but I'm coming up blank. That and she's pregnant. I have no fucking clue what pregnant women can take. I have never felt so useless in my life.

Lena moans into the sheets and the women completely ignore my question. Grace tilts the screen and holds the computer in front of me so I can see it. "Do this, Jude. Watch how he pushes on her hips. That might help her a bit with the pain." My little Alpha mate shows me a video of a man pushing against a woman's hips. I nod my head. I can do that. I can do this for my mate. I climb on the bed that groans with my weight and put my palms against her hips and push in, just like that guy was doing.

"Harder!" Lena moans into the pillow. She shocks me with her demand, but I instantly push her hips harder together. "Harder, please!" She whimpers. Shit. If I push into her hips any harder, they'll fucking break. I don't want to hurt her, but how can I ignore her? Before I have a chance to gauge the situation her body visibly relaxes.

"Okay, it's done." Lena's breathy voice cuts through me. This is really happening. Holy shit. I'm not fucking ready for this.

"Did your water break?"

Lena shakes her head, her damp hair clinging to her face as she does. I can barely believe this is happening as Grace asks her a series of questions in a calm and gentle voice. I barely register them speaking as I stare at my mate in a mix of terror and awe. She's going to have a baby. She's going to give birth to a baby. Lena's hand starts waving frantically before she buries her head into the pillow.

"Jude!" Grace smacks me on my shoulder and I stare at her. I have no fucking clue what to do. "Her hips!"

"Oh, oh. I got it. I got it." I put pressure on her hips again, good and hard. "That feel good?"

"No!" I let go thinking I hurt her, but she screams louder.

"Don't stop, please!" I put counter pressure on her hips again and wait for more instructions.

"What do I do?"

"You keep doing that. Everything's going to be fine." The young human then turns her attention back to Lena, "You're doing great Lena. You're really doing wonderful." I look at Lizzie like she's lost her damn mind. Nothing about this is wonderful.

"Done." Lena barely breathes the word, but I let up as soon as she does. I gently pat her back.

"What do you need?" She shakes her head at my question and swallows.

"Water."

"How about some ice? You don't want to get sick." Grace's voice comes out full of certainty. How the fuck could water make her sick? Lena nods in agreement and my Alpha mate is quick to leave.

Thank fuck for Grace and Lizzie, at least with them running this show I can concentrate on my mate. I only feel slight relief though. I take a look around the room and realize I'm the only one who's freaking out. Even Lena seems to be fine in between her contractions. All right. I concentrate on my breathing and the second Lena leans forward and pushes on her thighs I place my palms against her hips and push inward. Her head arches back and I feel her low moan vibrate down her spine.

I do not fucking like this. I should just leave. If I wasn't concerned that she's going to die any minute, I'd be out of that door in a heartbeat.

"You're doing great Lena. They're coming on close and you're taking them on perfectly. You'll be holding your little one soon." Lizzie's words calm Lena, but they do nothing to calm me. I'm not ready for this shit. I'm not even close to being prepared.

Grace comes into the room and stands by the bed as the contraction passes through Lena. "Here you go." Lena tries to grab the cup of ice, but her body sways and her hand goes back down to the mattress. I quickly grab her hips to steady her and gently rub her back.

The silver lining is that she isn't pushing me away. I hope I'm doing right by my mate. I hope I'm worthy in this moment.

Lizzie wipes the sweat from Lena's forehead while whispering calming words to her. "That's right. Just keep thinking that." My forehead pinches and my brows furrow in confusion. Lizzie can hear her? My heart skitters and I don't think I can breathe.

"You're doing so good Lena. That's right, you'll be holding your baby soon." I listen internally, but I can't hear a damn thing from either Lizzie or Lena. Lena hasn't bonded with the pack yet, or with me, so it makes sense that I'm not able to hear her. But how the hell can Lizzie hear her? And why can't I hear Lizzie? Caleb and Dom keep talking about how her wolf is hiding, but none of this makes sense.

"What's happening?" I ask Lizzie, but she only peers up at

me and tells me that everything is all right. "Don't be scared," she tells me, as if it's that easy. My mate... I can't help my mate and I don't have control.

Grace tilts the cup to Lena's lips and lets her take a few crushed cubes into her mouth. She hesitantly pulls the cup back and asks, "More?" Lena shakes her head and whispers a thank you as the door to my bedroom opens again.

"Oh good. It looks like I got here just in time." A little, red-headed witch walks into the room interrupting my thoughts. Her thin lips smile, making even more lines appear around her green eyes that are emphasized by a small pair of glasses. She radiates a calmness that puts me slightly at ease.

"Thank fuck you're here." As I sit back on my heels only now realizing the trembling of my hands, Lena yells into the mattress and I instantly pop back up to put pressure on her hips again. How long does this go on for?

"I'm here to help you, Lena," the witch says and brushes by me with a hint of a smile.

"Should we go?" Grace quietly asks Lizzie, but before Lizzie responds, Lena reaches out with a death grip and squeezes Lizzie's arm.

"Please don't leave me." Her strangled words might as well have been screamed.

"Okay Lena. We won't. I promise we won't." Lizzie gently pats Lena's hand through her contraction and Grace settles in her seat.

"A heating pad and labor oil will help." The little witch opens a huge black bag on the foot of the bed and digs through it for a box of gloves. "I'm going to have a look-see little wolf. Just stay right where you are." She pulls the gloves down her hands and releases them with a snap. The sound makes me flinch. I scoot to the side as the witch comes up from behind. "This may sting a bit." She drawls out the statement while moving her hands in between Lena's thighs.

I'm not fucking looking. Instead I stare at the ceiling and hold my breath.

For a moment, I consider leaving now that the healer's here, but I feel rooted to the bed. Lena moans in discomfort and I sit there helplessly although I try to ease her pain. I awkwardly push my palms against her hips as the doctor slowly moves away. I glance down and see blood on the healer's glove. Fuck, no. I can't fucking do this. As a lightheadedness washes over me, I hear a pop and a gush of liquid splashes across my thighs soaking my jeans. My brows shoot up and I simply stare down at my pants and then at Lena.

"Oh fuck." I groan without thinking. I hold my breath and say a silent prayer that this is over soon as another contraction distracts my mate.

"You're doing so good Lena." My mate shakes her head at Grace's words.

After a moment, she spits out "I can't" before moaning into the sheets. I take my cue and push against her hips, praying like fuck that I'm not making things worse.

"You can, dear, and you will soon. You're in transition." The witch's voice seems to calm my mate as her shoulders relax. "You'll get to hold your baby soon."

"Soon...like how soon?" I can't help but to ask. I really want this to be over with.

"However long it takes." The healer's answer is real fucking helpful.

IT FEELS LIKE HOURS GO BY, but every time I look at the clock it's only been about fifteen minutes. My poor mate is in so much pain. She's sweating, and after every contraction her head collapses back onto the mattress in exhaustion. Every contraction, every push, seems to be worse than the last. I feel like a little bitch because my hands and arms are fucking killing me from putting counter pressure on her hips, but she keeps begging me to push harder.

All the while, all I can think is that had I been sent any other day, what would have happened to her? All the ifs and worries race through my mind. Not a damn one is helping.

"One more push." The healer's words barely register with me as I watch Lena scrunch her face up as her body bears down. Lena falls against the mattress, and I see the healer lift her hands up from the corner of my eye. I turn to see Lena's baby in the healer's hands.

He's blue.

He can't be okay. Fuck, no. My body chills at the sight of him. My heart stops in my chest as I look at the tiny creature. His little body jiggles in an inhuman way as the healer unwraps the cord from his neck. Fuck. Fuck. My body goes numb. He's so blue. The healer reaches into his little mouth and then pats the baby on his butt.

He's wrinkly and blue and screaming.

He's screaming.

Blinking away the sadness, I listen to his squeal and Lena's cry of relief. That must mean he's okay. I wish the healer would fucking say something, instead she gently places the tiny baby on Lena's chest while his little fists ball and he continues to squeal. Lena wipes tears away from the corner of her eyes.

I'm paralyzed, merely watching and unsure what to do. My throat is dry and my wolf howls, pressing against my chest to go to them.

I stare at the women in the room, and they all have dreamy looks on their faces like this is normal. Tears well in my eyes and I just sit there waiting for someone to tell me he's okay. That Lena's okay. That whatever the fuck that was is over.

I look at the screaming little thing and stare in awe as his color changes with every breath. My lungs fill and it's only then that I realize I'd been holding my breath. The little pup calms down as Lena gently shushes him and cradles him close to her chest. Her eyes are glassy with tears, and she looks hysterical as her shoulders rock with a mixture of crying and laughter coming from her. She's fucking beautiful.

I'll remember this moment forever.

I don't know what the hell to do, but I know I want to hold her. Even if she can't feel our bond and my pull to her, maybe it will calm her a little if I hold her. Shit, maybe it will calm me down just to be close to her.

I crawl across the bed and slowly put my left arm above her head as I lay my body next to hers. She's staring at the baby in her arms and doesn't even seem to notice me. That's all right though because she's obviously at ease. That's all I want. I let my warmth settle around us and tell her that he's beautiful and that she did a great job. I'm only repeating what the women told her but still, it makes her smile and whether she knows it or not, she leans into me slightly.

I look down at the baby in her arms, he's calm and nuzzling into the crook of her arm. He's so small. So fragile. I'm surprised he's moving so much. Strong little thing. I look at his face and search for details of Lena, or...Shadow. The reminder shoots a cold wave through my blood. I look back at the baby expecting to feel resentment, but I feel nothing but relief and happiness. He's my mate's child. Therefore, he's my child.

My heart swells at the realization. I've barely wrapped my head around the fact that I've found my mate and now I have a son.

I can't help but wonder as I watch the two of them...if she now can feel our bond...or if she never will.

CHAPTER 5

JUDE

My heavy eyelids slowly open, sleep threatening to take me but I'm just not ready to give in. All of this is too new, too fragile, and I'm afraid to let go even if it is just to dream of them. Lena's finally asleep and the little one is squirming. I don't want him to wake her. She's been fussing over him and trying to get him to latch on to feed for hours before she finally dozed off. The little witch has left. Everyone is content that both Lena and the pup are healthy and well. Lena herself is already healing although a touch slower than wolves do. She needs to eat and to sleep, witch's orders.

Grace and Lizzie left first, shooed out by the witch hours ago. Lena thanked them all, although she hasn't said much to me. A whispered "thank you" when I readjust her pillow. A gentle "no thank you" when I've asked if there's anything I can do.

I don't know my place, other than beside her, waiting and ready for whatever is to come. I've watched the color return to her cheeks, her wounds heal, and sleep slowly restores her strength. And I keep waiting, hoping, that she'll feel the pull. I keep imagining the spark that will come to her eyes when I look down at her. But all it is at this point is a dream that keeps me from being able to rest.

With Lena soundly sleeping and the little one wriggling, I pick up her little boy with both hands, although I could probably carry him steadily with just one. He's so tiny. He opens his mouth to squeal, but I slip the tip of my pointer down his nose and across his upper lip and he latches right on. Just like he did with Lena. A small smile curls my lips up as I set him down on the makeshift cushion on my dresser.

Just yesterday morning, life was completely different. I never could have imagined this would be my life so soon.

I keep my left hand on his squirmy little body and grab the tiny-ass diaper and wipes with my right. Someone's bound to drop this squirmy little guy, but I'll be damned if it's going to be me. I chuckle to myself as I wipe his bottom, put the clean diaper on, and bundle him up like the little witch showed me. It doesn't look right, but he'll be fine. I sit with him in the rocker that Grace brought in earlier and stare down at the little guy; he's wriggling a bit as I try to rock him to sleep. I'll have to wake Lena if he gets any fussier since he might be hungry.

The very thought of doing that makes me nervous. She needs her rest and I don't want to wake her. I don't want to fail her at such a delicate time.

I've already done that tonight based on her little cries and short-lived sobs. I had to ask her what was wrong and in return she merely shook her head and refused to look at me. She's not well and I can't even hear her, I can't soothe her as a mate should.

I don't understand how Lizzie bonded with her before I did. How could she hear my mate when I hear nothing?

The thought eats at me in the night. As I stare down at her child though, our child, I'm reminded of how grateful I am that he waited to make an appearance until I got them here safely. My heart drops and my eyes travel along his face. I keep remembering that he's not mine. And it fucking kills me each time the thought comes to me. I look between Lena and her son. Her eyes are almond shaped with dark thick lashes, her lips are thin, but the bottom lip is lush. Her cheeks high and jaw narrow. He looks nothing like her. He looks just like Shadow. My jaw ticks and my fists clench. I fucking hate it. I have no right to claim this child as my own, but I'm damn well going to do it.

Shadow's a dead man. That's all he is. He's no father. He

had no right to claim my mate. This child is mine. Just like Lena is mine. A low growl grows in my throat but stops as I see Lena's body hunch forward in her sleep. I gently trail my fingers down her jaw and down farther to her neck. She's so beautiful. My eyes linger on the silver scar on her skin as I settle the baby and put him down. I'm going to fucking destroy that scar. I can't wait to ruin it with my own bite. At least three bites. And then I get the other side of her neck all to myself. The scars will be faint, but I want my bite to be clear and obvious to everyone. I don't want it mixed with his wrongful claim to her.

Sighing heavily, I run my hands through my buzzed hair and down my face. Shock and disbelief from all that happened has deprived me of sleep. Just last week I was mateless and without a care in the world. A smile widens across my face. Now I have a family. How the fuck did I get so damn lucky? My smile dims as I watch Lena turn in her sleep. She doesn't even know she's my mate. I'll tell her. It fucking hurts that I have to tell her because she feels nothing between us.

None of this should have happened this way. I don't know how she came to be Shadow's, but I'll slowly torture him if his claim has broken my mate's ability to feel our bond.

I always imagined my mate would feel this spark and pull, and I still have hope that in the morning she may feel the pull. With one last look at her beautiful form, her chest rising and falling with easy breaths, I quietly make my way to the door. The floorboard barely creaks and I pause, looking back and holding my breath before moving forward once again.

If I'm useful to her, surely she'll accept me even if she doesn't feel it. Nervousness creeps down the back of my neck along with the fear that is very real: she could deny me. After what she's been through, I could very well see that happening, and it didn't escape me when my pack brought up the possibility among themselves while I drove home in silence with her. Nothing like this has ever happened and I don't know what to expect.

Swallowing thickly, I make my way to the kitchen, ignoring every thought in the back of my mind. I'll grab her something to eat before I wake her. She's got to be hungry. She had a quick shower while I changed the sheets, but other than that she hasn't done anything but hold her son.

My bare feet smack on the tiled floor as I enter the kitchen with hollow hope. I shouldn't be surprised that I'm not the only one here. Lizzie and Grace pop their heads up from their bowls of cereal and smile brightly at me. Still in their pajamas, they've had little sleep if the bags under their eyes are anything to go by. A low chuckle escapes me.

"Morning."

"How are they doing?" I hear Lizzie's question as I open the door to the fridge. It soothes nearly every worry knowing how welcomed my mate is. They love her already and I fucking love them even more for it.

I grab the bottle of orange juice, not bothering with a glass, and take a few gulps before setting it on the counter to take it to Lena before answering, "They're doing good. They're both sleeping," I turn to peek at them. "So that's good right?" They both stand and gather around the island with dreamy eyes.

Grace nods her head. "Sleep is good." She glances at Lizzie before adding, "We have so much to do."

"We're going to throw Lena a baby shower!" Lizzie squeals.

"I know it's late, but she still deserves one. And then of course we have to set up the nursery. Unless she plans on keeping him in her room for a while. Well I guess either way we'll have to set it up." Grace continues rambling while I dig through the fridge for some fresh fruit and grab two cups of yogurt for her niece and nephew. I pause after closing the door. My niece and nephew.

Without hesitation I turn to them to ask, "Are the kids awake yet?"

"Not yet." It's odd the relief I feel knowing the two of them are keeping an eye on the little ones. "They need a shower bad. We have their rooms to set up, too."

Lizzie lets a hand fall to her tummy and my eyes follow the movement. I take in her scent without intention and raise my brows in surprise. I can already smell her pregnancy. More shock hits me. It's very early on, but the scent is strong. I don't think she even knows.

I wonder which one of her mates got her pregnant. Suppressing a laugh, I keep the next thought to myself: I don't want to be around when they find out. I scent the air again, but Grace isn't scenting any differently. It's early yet, so I just leave it be.

Clearing my throat, I go back to my task and listen to Grace rattle on. "Whatever you two think," I tell them and make it obvious that I am not staying to chat. I don't think I have much to offer in terms of décor and showers.

"You think we could make the living room into a playroom?" Grace spins on her heels as they continue to talk about adding onto the house and redecorating. I watch them walk out of the kitchen waving their hands in the air as they debate the merits of the color yellow for the playroom since it's a "happy" color.

Taking in the quick breakfast I nod, somewhat satisfied. I've got a couple hard-boiled eggs, an apple, yogurt, and orange juice. I don't know if she'll like any of it, but at least it's something. Before I can leave though, I find myself with company again. This time it's Devin.

I know it's him without having to look up. His footsteps are heavy and even. "We have to leave soon. We need to take care of Shadow's pack before they come for us or, more likely, before they run." His voice is low; he speaks with his eyes watching the doorway, making sure the women are out of hearing range.

I tap the bottle against the countertop. He's already dressed in black jeans and a black, long sleeved Henley. He's ready to act. Knowing my Alpha, he's been on edge and waiting since the moment I first told him.

He murmurs the question quietly and with caution, "Does she know?"

"No." I'm sure she's figured out that I'm going to kill Shadow and his pack. I don't think she'll object, but I'm not going to give her the chance. I don't like the thought of making her upset, but this is a done deal. He will never touch her again and the only way to ensure that is put him six feet in the ground.

"We need to speak to Alec first." My eyes widen in shock as they lock with his.

"You want their permission?" My tone is incredulous, and I know better than to speak to my Alpha like that, but he can't be serious. We don't ask for permission from the Authority. We never have and there's no need to now. This has nothing to do with interspecies relations. No one's going to miss these fuckers when we take them out.

"Not permission. No." Devin sits on the barstool, leans back, and crosses his arms. "Do you remember when we confronted Shadow's pack before?"

I nod. "Of course." Shadow's pack used to have claim to Shadow Falls, until Devin came back to fight for the territory.

It should've been his all along.

"And you said there were women there? Just like last time. Unwell." As I nod, I realize what he's getting at, and I attempt to remedy his concern.

"We'll leave them there. Someone else can deal with them." My words are hard and I don't have any sympathy for them. Not after watching them do nothing for those pups, for my niece and nephew. Devin nods his head, taking me by surprise.

"We will. And the Authority will be prepared to deal with it."

The hint of a smile from Devin meant to ease my worries works. A slow smirk pulls my lip up.

"Got it. So a quick stop at the Authority and then we can get this over with." A numbing cold shoots through me. As hungry as I am for revenge, I want this to be over with. I've hardly had any time with my mate. And she still has no idea what she means to me.

"Good. We leave now."

"But Lena—"

"She will be taken care of."

My lips part in protest but Devin adds, "It is probably best she has time to heal, and possibly that will help with ... your bonding."

I stop short, uncertain. "We're ready to go now, Jude," Devin tells me. "Grace already knows. She'll care for Lena and when we're home, after what must be done, the two of you will have a better chance."

I swallow the lump in my throat and pray that he's right.

I like Alec enough, he's all right, but I don't fucking trust him.

I don't really trust anyone for that matter, except my pack. And I don't know Alec enough to trust him or his word. He's had Devin's back on more than one occasion, so that gives him an edge over most people, but I still find myself uncomfortable in his office. I readjust in the seat, and it squeaks under my weight.

The practically ancient office sits upstairs in the Authority's estate and there's only one door. Which means only one way out. Clearing my throat, I stand from the leather upholstered seat to look out of the antique paned windows overlooking the grounds as we wait for Alec. Our estate is beautiful and refined. It's modern, built with every upgrade Devin could get, simply because he could. The Authority's property is ours on steroids with an antique touch.

There are a handful of witches testing their powers in the gardens below us. Hydrangea and rose bushes, I think, and maybe some other kind of flower, are lined perfectly in rows outlining a simple, rectangular fountain that's at least twenty feet long. A young witch keeps sputtering a blue light from her hands and hurling it into the still water. My hand grips a bit tighter on the edge of the sill. It does nothing; her shoulders sag with disappointment. I can't imagine what she's trying to do. I tilt my head as I continue to watch two witches talk animatedly even as I hear the door open.

Alec.

The knowledge of his presence makes me uneasy. Simply because the only exit is the one closest to him. He may be a member of the Authority, but he is not a member of our pack. I glance down to the ground from the window, we're stories up, but I could manage the drop if I had to. I trust Devin, but I still don't know Alec. Shit, even when you know people, they can turn their backs on you.

"I'm sorry to keep you waiting Devin," Alec starts before seeing me. "Ah. Jude. My apologies to you as well." I only nod in acknowledgment and stay by the window. Alec unbuttons his blazer and takes a heavy seat at the head of his desk. He runs a hand down his face in exasperation and I'm taken aback. I've never seen the sorcerer anything but calm and put together.

He's professional and if I'm honest, I've always thought of him to be stiff and lacking emotion. This is nothing like that.

Devin sits easily in one of the two seats across from him and is completely relaxed. I watch my Alpha carefully, but there are no signs of danger. He's at ease and I wish I could say the same. With my Alpha unguarded, my wolf raises his hackles. He's constantly on guard and untrusting. I take a seat on the edge of the chair and lean forward with my elbows on my knees. I just want to get this over with. I have a mate and a pup to return to. They were still sleeping when I left, and I didn't dare to wake them. Grace and Lizzie are listening for them. Thank God for those two. Veronica and Vince should be back to the estate soon and then Dom, Caleb and Lev will join us for the attack. My fists clench and I crack my knuckles.

"Long day?" Devin questions.

"You have no idea. Please tell me I don't need to torture or kill any other members of the Authority."

Devin chuckles and I find myself smirking along with him. "Not that I know of. We just wanted to give you a little heads up."

Alec's brow cocks as he sighs. "What are you going to do this time Devin?" This time I chuckle along with Devin.

"We have to retaliate. We're going today to take down Shadow's pack."

"Take down?" Alec finally straightens in his seat.

Devin cracks his neck before answering. "We're going to kill Shadow, that's long overdue. Anyone who surrenders we plan to leave behind."

Alec nods his head slowly while resting his elbows on the desk, clasps his hands, and his thumbs rub back and forth against one another before his eyes find Devin's. "How many do you think?" Devin doesn't answer, he simply looks at me expectantly.

"There were four women, including Shadow's mate. I doubt they'll fight." Alec nods his head again. "They were not in their right minds, high from the looks of it, the entire time I was there."

"We don't want any backlash from the Authority." Devin's words come out harder than I expect.

"No need to worry. I can't imagine anyone would object. As you said, it's long overdue." Devin nods his head and starts to respond, but a knock at the door stops him.

Just as Alec lifts his head to answer the knock, the door parts and a small blonde human walks in. Curiosity causes me to glance between her and Alec. She holds onto her fingertips and nervously pinches them as she walks with uncertainty toward Alec. Her eyes don't roam the room; she doesn't bother with us at all. Alec clears his throat and looks pointedly at us, as if alerting her of our presence. She stops a foot away from the desk and parts her lips before looking over her shoulder at us. Her mouth closes and her eyes linger on the floor.

"Bella?" At Alec's soft call, her eyes raise to his and glimmer with hope. A small smile makes her cheeks rise, but it holds a hint of sadness.

"I—" She stutters and watches her fingers as she nervously plays with them again. Finally, her shoulders square and she meets Alec's gaze. "I was wondering if you'd like any tea."

"I'm fine. Thank you. Devin? Jude?" Alec doesn't look at us as he asks. Concern is written on his face as he continues to stare at the beautiful woman. There's obviously something there, but it's a delicate matter. I shake my head and keep my nose out of it. That's none of my fucking business.

Devin rests his left elbow on the arm of his chair and leans so he can take his chin in his hand and watch the scene while shaking his head at Alec's offer. "No, thank you."

Bella, as Alec called her, nods slightly before turning to face us for the first time. Her eyes catch sight of me, and she instantly brightens, as though whatever was plaguing her has vanished. "You're Jude!" Goosebumps flow down my arms and I still at her words. Who the hell is she? I scent the air again and confirm that she's human. As I glance at Devin, whose expression indicates he's unaware of who she is as well, she asks me, "How's your mate? She will do great things for your pack."

"What kind of things?" Devin asks as I stare down the cute, little blonde. She has an innocence about her that's undeniable. But she also radiates happiness with her bright brown eyes and wide smile. Her teeth are perfect, and her pale skin only adds to her beauty.

"Not your pack...Jude's pack." The crease on my forehead deepens at her words. She's confused. Or delusional.

"Devin is the Alpha of my pack." I speak clearly and confidently. I have no desire to challenge him, and I don't want there to be any question about that.

"Oh, you haven't seen your brothers yet, have you?" She

tilts her head while speaking to me as though she pities me. There's an otherworldly absence to her in this moment. Something that gives me chills. I don't need her pity, but what the fuck does she know about my brothers? My heart beats chaotically, remembering what the seers told my father long ago. The seers envisioned one of us, either myself or my brothers, killing our father. Hearing this little woman talk about his pack as if it's my own, it churns a sickness in my stomach.

But I shut that shit down; seers are liars.

Before I have a chance to ask, she answers my question, "Don't worry, they're fine. Well, they have their hands full with their mate at the moment." She turns toward Alec and smiles.

"Their mate?" I can't help but question. "One mate...for both of them?"

The little blonde practically rolls her eyes. "They're not very good at sharing, but I guess they're trying." The knowledge that my brothers are mated forces a smile from me. Emotions swarm but I remain calm on the exterior. My brothers have a mate. And now so do I. My throat dries a bit too quickly and I clear it once again.

It's been years since I've seen them, but to know they're doing well fills my chest with pride and happiness. Occasionally we speak, but it's been a long time since any of us has reached out to one another.

A huff of a laugh leaves me as I finally lean back in the

seat and cross my arms. Fate gave them a mate to share. What a bitch.

"So you haven't seen them yet?"

I only shake my head at her question.

"Well they'll be needing your help soon."

"Why is that?" I don't know who she is, and just like Alec, I don't trust her.

"It seems your father is getting himself into a bit of trouble." Hearing her talk about my father makes my blood run cold. Any semblance of a smile disappears instantly from my face.

"That's enough Bella." Alec's stern scolding wipes the happiness from Bella's face as she nods slightly.

I glance between the two of them before stating calmly, "I have no business with my father and neither do they."

She only offers a small smile that doesn't reach her eyes, nods, and says, "Of course."

"I would know." I attempt to reassure her and stop myself from giving my true opinion about the seers.

In response, Bella merely walks to Alec's side after forcing another small smile for me and gives Alec a kiss on the cheek, taking all of us by surprise. As she opens the door to leave, she turns halfway to face me. "Maybe you should pay your father a visit and see what your pack has become."

CHAPTER 6

JUDE

"I want Shadow." My darkly spoken words break up the laughter coming from the back of the SUV. Dom, Caleb, and Lev are in the back and Lev is fucking around as usual. Devin's driving and he doesn't hesitate to nod his head.

Devin answers, "I should've ended him the second I took Shadow Falls back."

My fists clench and my jaw ticks. Had Devin sought justice when he returned to Shadow Falls years ago to reclaim his family's territory, I have no idea how I would've ever found my mate. But there's no doubt in my mind she wouldn't have suffered like she has these past years.

"We'll park a ways out and split up." Devin's eyes focus on

the rearview mirror. "You three go to the left; Jude and I will go to the right."

"How many are we up against?" Lev asks from the back. The SUV jostles as Devin turns to drive off the road.

"Four women who probably won't do shit but scream and run and four men. So we're equal in number."

"No kids this time, though. So there's no reason to show any mercy." Devin adds and I nod my head. The car shifts over a bump and I sway numbly remembering the last time. The children prevented us from slaughtering all of them. Devin's right. There's no reason to hold back now. This ends today once and for all.

"Let's make this fast. I want to go home to my mate." I grit my teeth and look out the window. As we get closer to our target, my heart races faster and faster. I've never been more eager for anything in my life. I decide to lighten the mood and my gaze shifts to the rearview mirror. "I'm surprised you two left your mate."

"Why is that?" Caleb grins wide. He's so damn proud of Lizzie. Even Dom, the hulking beast who hasn't said shit the entire time we've been in here, breaks out a hint of a smile.

"Now that she's knocked up, I didn't think you'd leave her."

Both Caleb and Dom look shocked at my words, genuinely so. Neither speaks although Caleb's bottom lip drops. "You've gotta be shitting me."

I turn in my seat to stare at them. "How the fuck didn't

you smell that?" It's early, but she scented strong of pregnancy. I start to doubt myself.

"Don't fuck with us." Dom sounds pissed, but he always sounds pissed.

I hold up both my hands. "Not fucking with you. Congrats to both of you."

They look at each other as though they're sizing the other one up. I smirk at their possessive reaction.

"Definitely my pup." Caleb grins cockily. Dom crosses his arms and snorts.

The moment is quickly extinguished as the car slows on a gravel road. "Game time, gentlemen."

Devin finally parks and we all get out. The car is relatively hidden, but we're still a mile away so it doesn't entirely matter. It's late, dark, and we have the advantage of sneaking up on them. But I am not naïve, they have to know something is coming. I imagine they're on edge. Truthfully, we won't know what we're up against until we're there.

We follow Devin's lead and take off our clothes and leave them behind; no sense in shredding them. After tossing them into the back of the car, I walk a few steps into the forest barefoot and shift. The feeling is exhilarating as my wolf takes form. My bones bend and crack as they morph into a beast of a creature. My skin stretches taught, sending a familiar and quick burning sensation over my entire body as fur grows in its place. Within seconds my wolf has taken over. My wolf snarls, knowing we're approaching the enemy. Although he's relieved to finally get vengeance, to be able to act, he allows me to lead. I shake out my body, feeling my stiff joints loosen as I quietly stalk deeper into the forest.

"Keep him quiet, Jude." I nod my head at Devin's command. I scold my wolf, but he doesn't give a shit. The only thing on his mind is ripping Shadow's throat out. He pictures it over and over again as we move silently through the trees.

With each step and with every crack of a branch beneath me, my eagerness grows. We're quiet as we approach. Each of us moving into place and in pace with one another. So much like last time, yet this time, so much more is at stake.

As the moonlight filters down and the sounds of camp can be heard, adrenaline flows faster and harder in my veins.

I huff in disbelief as we approach the tree line. A drunken male holds a shotgun lazily in one arm while he takes a swig of whiskey. Two men are around the fire eating as though nothing has happened. "Your turn next fucker," the man with the gun calls over his shoulder, "then I get to eat."

"Are they fucking serious?" I speak only in my head as do the other members of my pack. I can't believe this is how Shadow's pack has responded. They had to have fucking known we were coming.

"Don't let your guard down; this could be a setup." My wolf lets out a low growl as Shadow leaves a hut just twenty feet in front of us. He takes his limp dick out and pisses into the woods, without a fucking care in the world.

I try to hold my wolf back. I want to wait for Devin's orders. But the need to rip the limbs from Shadow's body and claw at him until he's nothing but a lifeless pile of shredded flesh overwhelms me. My wolf pictures it and curls his lip back to reveal his fangs. His paws dig into the dirt as I fight the urgency building inside of him. His nostrils flare and a snarl rips through him as he overpowers my desire to wait until the order is given.

My limbs burn as I sprint in the woods over thick tree branches. The rough pads of my paws scrape against the debris. But I don't care. My wolf doesn't even feel the pain. I'm barely even aware of the screams and growls and barks. "Jude!" My pack screams at me to stop and to wait but I can't. The blood rushes loudly in my ears and all I can see is Shadow and the vision of him lying dead on the ground. It's a very near future for him that I'm happy to deliver.

With one last leap, I pounce as he turns to face the sudden ruckus from the woods. In nothing but ripped jeans, he faces me, his cock still in his hand.

A look of pure fear flashes across his face as I tackle him. My paws land hard on his chest, my claws dig into his flesh. He attempts to shift, but he's far too late.

Screams and snarls surround me, but I ignore them. I see nothing but red. My jowls widen and clamp down over the crook of his neck. Hot blood pours into my mouth as his jugular is slashed by my fangs. His strangled cry pierces through my ears. The claws that have morphed from his hands dig into my back. But he's weakened. Although I feel him battering against me, his fight is gone. I clamp down harder and then viciously tear at his throat. My claws slice through his skin as my wolf continues to maul him.

A hard body pushes against me, but I don't budge. My body is stone and every action vicious. My wolf howls in both victory and pain. In a flash Caleb is behind me and the yelp following indicates the demise of whoever it was that heedlessly tried to defend this piece-of-shit wolf. Shadow's pulse dims as my wolf snarls and takes a chunk of his throat in our jaws. I spit the filthy blood from my mouth.

A menacing growl rumbles from my chest as I turn to look at the state of this pathetic pack.

"No!" A shrill cry comes from the thin lips of Shadow's mate.

"Ah fuck, I didn't want to kill a woman." Dom mutters in my head as Shadow's mate shifts into a mangy looking mutt. Dom's wolf pounces, his paws landing on her shoulders. She falls helplessly as he pins her to the ground. He growls into her ear as a warning, but she still fights, nipping and snapping her jaws. Her teeth puncture his ear, and he snarls a greater threat. She barks loudly over and over, but her pack is silent.

Slowly, I rise from the corpse and take in what's happened while I attempt to breathe and steady myself.

From my place at the edge of the woods I can easily see

everything. Two wolves lie dead. One at the feet of Caleb and the other a few feet behind Devin. Dom has the Alpha mate pinned and the last remaining man, the one with a shotgun at his feet, and the three women are standing with wide eyes by the fire pit. The man has his hands raised in surrender and the front of his pants are soaked in urine. He didn't even attempt to shift. The women are shaking, and one is rocking back and forth crying hysterically. This is so fucked.

"Are they really fucking surrendering?" I sneer in my head. I find it hard to believe that the fight is already over. There's no surprise waiting for us. This wasn't enough. My wolf paces in a small circle. He snarls and barks with agitation. My mate. What they did to my mate comes back in flashes. My wolf isn't over it. There needs to be more. He tries to go back to the lifeless body, but I pull him away. This wasn't nearly enough to rectify the pain Shadow has caused me. Let alone the hell he put Lena through.

"Please don't hurt us." One of the women finally speaks. She sniffles and grabs hold of her shoulders. She's a pitiful sight. Her eyes are bloodshot, and her body shakes with every movement she makes. I'm not sure if it's from fear or from whatever high she's on.

My Alpha shifts. I'm momentarily surprised that he would shift to his weaker form and show such vulnerability. But then I take another look around. There's nothing here that's even close to a threat.

It's sickening. Both the disgust and the guilt. A pack with no Alpha, surely one left in this condition, is pathetic and in need of great help. Devin was right to alert the Authority.

"Tie up your Alpha mate." He commands the man and in an instant Dom releases her. She slashes out at him and snarls. The man looks back at Devin with an expression of equal confusion and fear. "Now!" Devin commands him and the Alpha waves rock through the camp. The women all fall to the ground and the man's legs weaken as he looks furiously around the camp for something to restrain the Alpha mate. She rises on her legs and attempts another futile attack. Dom merely swipes his heavy paw at her body as she leaps in the air. She crashes to the ground from the blow and her wolf gives in, shifting back to human.

"I don't fight women, Devin." Dom's voice is low and sorrowful in our heads.

Devin doesn't even bother shifting. His feet pound against the dirt as he walks with purpose to the Alpha mate, still partially stunned from the fall and naked in human form. His large hand grips her nape and pushes her head into the ground. The shifter from the other pack approaches quickly with rope in his hand, but I don't give him a chance to get anywhere near my Alpha. I barrel toward him, snarling and practically foaming at the mouth for another fight. He screams in terror and drops the rope as he falls to his ass in the dirt.

I pick up the rope in my mouth and turn my back to the

bastard. Showing him he means nothing to me. He's not worth my energy. Devin huffs a laugh and takes the rope in his other hand while the woman struggles beneath him. I shift and help him tie her to the tree to keep her from attacking us. More so we don't have to kill her. We'll leave her here for the Authority.

All the while she screams and cries "Shadow" while attempting to buck. Her effort is futile.

Once she's secure, Devin tugs on the rope and nods before turning back to the silent spectators. Everyone is in human form; the pathetic battle is over. My wolf howls with discontent, but I remind him that our mate is waiting for us. He shuffles and paces with impatience. I feel the same as my wolf. This wasn't a hard enough battle. I look back at Shadow, wishing I'd restrained my wolf and given him time to shift so I could've enjoyed the fight. My only regret is that he barely had a moment to suffer.

"Stay." Devin speaks to the enemy pack and stalks back to the woods, not waiting for them to frantically nod their heads in submission. Their fear and anxiety mix with the scent of blood and urine. The stench is nauseating. Our pack follows Devin into the woods, listening intently to ensure their obedience.

Devin pulls out his phone as he unlocks the SUV for us to pile in. "Alec." He puts the keys in the ignition before looking back through the forest at what's left of Shadow's pathetic pack. "They're all yours."

CHAPTER 7

JUDE

Hours with the hum of the SUV driving us home allow the adrenaline to fade. Half my pack slept the last hour, but I couldn't. The late night is nearly early morning by the time we're back. I'm so fucking tired, but the thought of my mate waiting for me gives me the energy I need. I walk quietly down the hall to my bedroom, cringing every time the damn wooden floor squeaks beneath my heavy weight. I try angling my boots and walking a bit slower. If they're asleep, I don't want to disturb them.

I turn the knob gently and slowly, pushing on the door with a slight weight to prevent too much sound. I haven't snuck around like this in years. I hold back a chuckle as I remember my brothers and I sneaking around the house at night to steal candy from the kitchen. Warmth fills my chest at the thought of my own pups doing the same, at the memory of family, and at knowing that the worst is truly behind us. An asymmetric grin pulls at my lips. I already have one pup; I can't wait to have more with Lena.

By the time I've broken into my own bedroom, I can't hear a damn thing in the room and it's pitch black with the curtains closed, but I can make out a small form bunched under the cream comforter on the bed. My mate. The sight makes my heart swell and my wolf brushes against my chest desperate to feel her. I've dreamed of coming home to my mate for as long as I can remember. Dreamed of climbing into bed behind her and pulling her small body into my chest. I can imagine the pleased sigh escaping her lips in her sleep. A soft rumble grows in my chest at the thought.

It feels as if I've already loved her for a lifetime.

My wolf is eager to climb into bed beside her, especially after the day we've had. I strip out of my filthy clothes as I silently stalk toward the bed. I know I need to shower first, but I just want to see her. After throwing on a pair of gray sweatpants, I slowly pull the covers back and frown as my blood turns cold and my fists bunch the comforter in my hand. Finally, I rip the damn thing away. It's empty. She's not in my room. For a moment, panic washes through me.

I scent the air and follow her sweet citrus smell to the door and down the hall. Not giving a damn about the smacking sound of my feet on the floor, I hunt her down. I'm led to the other side of the estate, and I let out a long, agitated sigh as I quietly open the door to her niece and nephew's room. Panic vanishes, but a mix of other emotions quickly take its place.

What the hell is she doing in here? My brow furrows in confusion and then harder in anger. She's my mate and she belongs in my bed. Tension rises up my shoulders and I do my best to keep my breathing even and stay firm in my place. I don't want to startle her, but I don't know what to do with all of the emotion that riddles its way through me. The loss of what could have been, if only I'd met her long ago before any of this shit happened.

I silently scold myself and cuss under my breath. I need to rectify that right fucking now. She's my mate whether she feels the pull to me or not. And I need to fucking act like it.

The door squeaks behind me as it opens just slightly and I hold my breath, hoping I haven't disturbed the children. My eyes adjust to the darkened night and any anger dissipates.

Some of the tension leaves my body as I see her curled behind her niece, her arm wrapped around the young pup. To the right of her is a bassinet, holding our sleeping pup. Everyone's sleeping soundly. I can't help the warmth that flows through me, even if I'm upset that she didn't stay in my bedroom. I can't blame her for wanting to be with her family.

But I'm her family now. My wolf howls in agony. The

feeling of loss and rejection is undeniable.

My throat dries and I struggle with what to do. Finally, after a moment of my heart racing and far too many old wounds reopening, I do what feels right.

I walk quietly across the room and gently peel the covers from around her body. I lift her arm from around her niece and tuck the blanket under the little girl. I slide my hands under my mate's soft, warm body and gently lift her. At the movement, her eyelids pop open and stare back at me in fear. It fucking kills me. It's a dagger to my already wounded heart. It takes everything in me to ignore the look and lean down to give her a small kiss on the tip of her nose as I carry her away from the room. Her body shifts in my arms as she reaches back for her son.

"He'll be fine." I whisper the words and shift her weight onto one arm and cup her ass in my hand while I brace her back with my arm. Carefully, I gently close the door and glance down at my little mate. The feel of her plump ass in my hand and her warm body against my chest has my dick hardening with need. But the expression on her face makes me second guess my lust for her. Her eyes stare blankly across the hall, shining with fear. I can feel her heart beating frantically and my wolf hates everything about this.

Her shoulders hunch with her arms crossed, shielding herself from me. She's wearing a nightgown that must belong to either Lizzie or Grace The thin cloth does nothing to offer her warmth. My pace quickens to get her to bed, to the privacy of our room, so we can talk and I can explain. So I can just have a chance to repair what's been done. She must feel my eyes on her. Her teeth sink into her bottom lip as she tilts her head down and slightly leans into me. Her entire body is tense and I fucking hate it.

This isn't the way it's supposed to be. Can't she feel this pull? This need? My entire being feels as if it's shattering. I don't know how I'm even standing with the pain that runs through me.

A knot grows and twists in my chest as I carry her to the bedroom. Our bedroom. We need to have a talk. I need to make it very clear that she's my mate. I'm slow to place her on the bed, a part of me fearing what she'll say when I tell her she's my mate, and that I was made to love her and she was made to love me. Because it's far too obvious, she doesn't love me in the least.

I watch as she slowly lifts her knees to her chest, still looking away from me. For the first time I realize she has absolutely no feelings toward me but fear. I can tell she's on the verge of tears and she doesn't know what to do and it fucking kills me. My chest rises as I take a heavy breath. My hands tremble, I've never felt this way. Not since I was a pup when everything happened back then...

I grind my teeth thinking of that fucking bastard Shadow and the fact that his bite has taken that away from me.

She really can't feel a pull to me. Not at all.

The bitter absolution makes my chest collapse. I close my eyes and try to gather my thoughts. I have my mate. I told her she belongs to me. She should know what that means. She should know what she means to me. The bed groans as I sit on the edge of it and wrap an arm around her waist to bring her closer to me.

"I expected you to be here when I came home." Her large hazel eyes finally meet mine as my low voice breaks the silence. "I wanted to hold you." Her eyes stay on mine as she nods slightly.

"I'm sorry. It won't happen again." I stare at her, wishing I'd spoken differently. I'm not admonishing her. I soften my voice even more.

"It's all right, baby. I have you now." I lean down to kiss her lips and she pulls away slightly before tilting her chin up so I can take her lips with mine. I nip her bottom lip and cup her chin in my large hand. Warmth wraps its way around me. Can she feel this? My heart stutters praying that she can.

As I pull away, I rub my thumb across her bottom lip. Her lips are so soft and plump. I lick my own wanting more, but I'm worried she isn't ready. Her eyes are still closed and her body leans toward me. Please, please, feel this. The spark that ignites inside of me is everything. Her breath comes in shallow pants, making her breasts rise slightly in the white cotton nightgown. My eyes travel down her body and I stroke my hardening dick.

"You should know better than to leave my bed." I growl into her ear as I push my body against hers down onto the mattress. My lips push against hers and lick her seam for her to open for me. A rumble of approval erupts from my chest as she obeys me and gives me entry. Fuck yes. My skin heats as my hands roam her body. My fingers tickle down the dip above her hips before grabbing her ass and pushing her farther up the bed. Her nipples are hard and poking through the fabric of her nightdress. The sight of her breasts bouncing with the movement makes me leak precum.

I crawl to her, stalking my little mate. Her eyes are still closed, and I will her to open them, but she doesn't. I let out a low, warning growl and her hazel eyes instantly find mine. I crawl between her legs, caging her body in with mine as I hover above her small frame. I plant my forearms on either side of her head and bump my hips against hers, letting my dick settle in between her legs. I can feel her heat against me and it feels like fucking heaven.

She should be fully healed by now. Thank fuck my mate's a shifter. I don't want to wait. I want her right now. I have to ask though, I'll be damned if I ever hurt her, "Are you all right?"

She doesn't waste any time shaking her head. Her lips form a small frown and her breath hitches. "I'm still sore." Her voice is hesitant and uncertain. It's more than obvious that she's lying.

My eyes narrow as I search her face for the reason she would lie to me. I shake my head at that thought. No, she wouldn't lie. Maybe she's still healing. That could be. I pull back and sit on my heels with my dick standing up right.

"I understand baby, turn over for me." I can still give her pleasure. I feel a small smile grow on my face. I'll need to be gentle, but she'll feel good. She'll feel more of this pull then. She must feel something.

She turns her body over onto her forearm and knees, lowering her upper half so that her chest is pressed into the mattress with her head facing away from me and her ass in the air. Her submission makes my dick throb with the desire to claim her, and I have to stifle my groan.

Fuck. My wolf howls with the need to feel hers. To be with hers. To be with our soul mates. My forever is so close, it taunts me.

I watch as her body trembles and a soft sob escapes her. The sight and sound make my heart still in my chest. What the fuck? My hands grow numb as my mate cowers from me.

I freeze. My entire being freezes. A beat passes and then another. She's not all right in more than just one way. My mate. My poor mate.

"Why are you crying?" I try to keep my voice even, but the concern is evident.

"I'm sorry I disappointed you." What the fuck just happened? I replay everything in my head, but I have no damn clue why she's in tears.

Slowly, I gently place my hand on her hip as I move to lie down on the bed, my chest against her side, before rolling her body into mine. She buries her head into my chest so I can't see her. "You didn't disappoint me, baby." I pull away and move my hand to her cheek, wiping the tears from her reddened face. I lower my forehead to hers and nuzzle my nose against hers. With my eyes closed, I kiss the tip of her nose. "Stop crying, you didn't disappoint me. What made you think that?"

"Because you told me to get into position." She stares at my chest as she softly speaks the words.

"Into position?" What the hell is she talking about? Her lips part, but she hesitates to speak. "Tell me what you mean."

"For punishment." Her hot breath tickles my chest as her words hit me with a force that makes my blood pound with rage. Sickness rises through me. An eternity in hell will not be enough for Shadow.

"Getting on your knees for punishment?" I barely hold on to my composure at this point. My bottom lip trembles as my body goes numb. I need to hear her say it. I want her to tell me so I know for sure. My blood is rushing in my ears and my muscles coil at the tension in my body.

"Yes, sir."

"Don't call me sir." I bite the hard words out and immediately regret them as she flinches. With steadying breath, I ask her what I must so I understand. Did he have you call him sir?" She noticeably swallows as she stares straight into my chest and nods before whispering a small "yes."

"I'm not him. I'm not Shadow. I'm your true mate." My heated, firm words have her eyes flying to meet mine. Her lips part, but she slams them shut before lowering her eyes to my chest once again and nodding. It's a nod of obedience, not acceptance.

The words have left me. The absolute truth... and she doesn't believe me. Any hope I had is gone and I question what I've done just now. I thought she felt it.

My hand wraps gently around her throat before traveling to her chin to lift her eyes to meet mine. I stare into her eyes, pleading for her to feel it. To feel an ounce of what I feel toward her. If she could feel this way, this love and devotion, the past pains would wane. I know they would. I can ease so much pain and take it from her. It's all I want. To give her a beautiful life.

"You are my mate. I feel the pull to you." I swallow thickly as she says nothing. I don't even know if she believes me. "Do you feel anything for me?" Her eyes soften as she searches my silver gaze. Tears brim in her eyes as she shakes her head no. My nostrils flare in anger, not at her, not at all, only because she has no pull to me whatsoever. I was a fool to think fate would have mercy on me after what I was put through as a pup.

"He had no rights to you. You. Are. Mine." I growl out

the words, barely containing my need to claim her right now. The full moon is still days away, but my need to sink my teeth into her skin, over that unrighteous mark, overwhelms all my other senses.

Her lower lip wobbles and I can tell she wants to say something, but she's holding back. "Tell me." It's a command, one that resonates from deep inside of me, from a place I've never felt before, and she dutifully obeys. It makes me feel like a piece of shit. She's obeying because that's what she's been trained to do. What he trained her to do.

"He had a pull to me as well."

"Bullshit!" I jump out of the bed and run my hands through my hair as I watch her shrink into the mattress away from me. Fuck! Heat races through me as my head spins. I need to get a grip. I run my hands down my face and lower myself to my knees in front of her. God help me. Someone fucking help me. I'm only making this worse. I need to fucking calm down so I stop frightening her.

"I'm sorry," I whisper as quickly as I can. "I'm not angry at you." Lifting my head, I find her eyes piercing into mine. I sigh heavily and stare at my mate trying to reflect my compassion and praying for her to understand. "I shouldn't have yelled. I hate that I yelled. I'm sorry." She nods, watching me as if she doesn't know what to make of me.

Attempting to silence the rage, I sit back on the edge of the bed. She doesn't move away from me, and I take my time, gently placing my hand on her leg, rubbing small circles on the tender skin on her thigh. She still hasn't moved, and I can't help but to think she's learned that behavior. To simply not move when faced with aggression. It sickens me.

"I want you here. I want you to tell me everything." I pat my thigh and she nods in understanding. I help her, pulling her into my lap and nuzzling my head into the crook of her neck, planting a soft small kiss there.

I breathe slowly, just holding her and letting the feeling of my mate in my lap calm me. I pull her back against my chest and sit her ass against my dick. My erection hasn't gone down for a single moment. It can't with the full moon so close and my mate so near. My rage has only fueled my need. But I'm not going to give in to it. Not like this. "Please forgive my outburst."

"I forgive you." Her words come out instantly and again I get the feeling that it's a learned behavior. It makes my heart crumple in my chest. I press my lips together to avoid questioning her. I need time to figure out how the hell I'm going to help my sweet little mate and convince her that my pull to her exists and it's real. Not like the fucking lie that Shadow fed to her.

"Can we talk another time?" she asks, at first staring ahead, but in my silence, she peers up at me. "I'm tired and I have a lot to think about."

My heart beats hard against my chest and she glances down, as if she felt it or heard it. A glimmer of hope torments me, wanting me to believe she can feel the pull.

I swallow the lump in my throat and tell her "of course" even though every second that passes draws a deeper gouge into my agony.

"I'm going to take a shower." I whisper the words into her neck and gently set her on the bed next to me. Her lips part, but again slam shut. I close my eyes in anguish. She won't even talk to me. She feels the need to censor herself and I don't like it. "What?" I open my eyes and give her a small, forced smile. "Tell me whatever it is."

Her eyes dart to the floor and then back to mine. "Can I set up the baby monitor? Is that okay?" Her voice is so small and full of defeat. As though I'd deny her that request. I shake my head at my stupidity. Of course I should have thought of that.

"Did you get one today?"

"Grace and Lizzie brought me more things for the baby." She keeps her head down as she speaks and I fucking hate it. I'm ashamed that her submission turned me on in the least.

"Have you decided what you're going to call him?" I try to lighten the conversation, but my voice is uneven as I push the words out.

"No." Her fingers play with the hem of her nightgown with nervousness. I only nod my head and look past her at the door to the bathroom. I need some fucking distance to wrap my head around all this shit.

"Do you need anything else?"

I fucking hope the answer is yes so I can give her whatever it is that she needs, but she shakes her head and barely speaks, "No, s—"

My jaw ticks as she stops herself from saying "sir."

She twists her fingers in her hand as she realizes her mistake. I decide to ignore it and not bring any more attention to it. "Do you need any help?" I bristle with anger and tension toward myself and I'm doing a shitty job at hiding either of them from my scared mate.

She shakes her head but at least meets my eyes. "Okay then. Go ahead and set up whatever you need." I walk around the bed to the bathroom, but I don't fucking breathe until I close the door. I want to pound my fist into the wall, but that'll only scare her even more. Fuck! I turn the shower on but keep the temperature low. I need to cool down. I stand with both hands against the wall as the water hits the back of my head and my back, dripping down my face and falling off my lips onto the floor. What the fuck am I going to do?

I've told her she's my mate and she doesn't believe me. Tears of anger and despair prick my eyes. She frightened of me and afraid to do anything because she thinks she'll disappoint me. Fuck! My hand balls into a fist and I'm desperate to let out every emotion that brings me to my knees. It's a death you're forced to live through when a mate denies you.

I wish I could take out all of this anger onto that piece-of-shit shifter. His lifeless body flashes before my eyes. I ball my hand into a fist and slam it against the wall as a snarl leaves my chest. The tiles crack at the impact, leaving blood and shattered pieces of marble to fall to the floor. She can probably hear it, but the release is exactly what I need. I keep myself from doing it again and again like I really fucking want to. I lean my head back, close my eyes, and let the water splash on my face as I feel my hand heal.

When I open my eyes I spot several bottles of girly shit. Slowly, the emotions calm.

Grace or Lizzie must've got her something to wash up with. I flip the top cap open and see it's been used. She accepts help from them.

She trusts them. She's bonded with them. Hell, she heard Lizzie...even if it was out of desperation. There is hope; she just needs to get comfortable here. And with me. I sniff the bottle and quickly put it back. I prefer her natural smell better, but if she wants to use this shit that's fine with me.

I convince myself that she'll feel a pull to me at some point. Hopefully once I claim her, my essence should outweigh his. After all, I'm her rightful mate. Although, I honestly have no idea how it works. I've never known a wolf to claim an already claimed mate. My heart stills and my blood runs cold. I better still be able to claim her.

Fear makes my breath come up short as I leave the stall and fist the towel in my hand. She's mine to claim. It'll destroy me if my bite is useless to her. I dry off in a rush as a panic sets in. The need to hold my mate is all consuming. My wolf whines in my chest until I open the door and see her lying under the covers on her side staring at the monitor on the nightstand. She watches me as I cross the room and walk with hard, determined strides to be by her side. I don't waste any time to lie behind her and kiss her exposed neck. It's the side that's untouched. The side that will bear my mark.

I look at the monitor and a genuine, although sad, smile plays at my lips. There's a tiny screen showing the sleeping pup in the cradle and a bar of green light at the top. Soft white noise bellows from the little machine. He's so small on the screen. Wrapped up tight in the thin, little blanket. He has more hair on an infant than I've ever seen and it's all black and thick. He may have his father's features, but he's so serene and fragile looking that I fail to see Shadow in his sweet little face at all.

I pull her closer to me, but with distance for her sake, and whisper into her ear, "You did good, baby." A beat passes and she says nothing, but her body molds against mine as a happy sigh leaves her lips and her fingertips gently touch the screen. She's far more relaxed and happier now that she can see her son. I give her jaw a small kiss and pull back the covers. I still think she'll feel our bond if only she'd let me in. And I'm determined to start tonight.

"Will you trust me for just a moment?" I ask her in a whisper. I'm quick to add, "I won't ever hurt you."

The cords in her neck tighten as she swallows and then agrees, "Yes, I'll trust you."

My heart pounds with uncertainty.

"Lie back and part your legs for me." I whisper the words and nip her earlobe before moving from behind her to give her room to do as I say. Her smile fades at my command, and I almost regret speaking. But she needs this. She needs to learn that I will give her pleasure without taking anything from her. That I will be selfless and love her even if she doesn't love me. And I'm going to give her that reason right now.

"If you want me to stop, say so," I tell her, and she nods in understanding but doesn't say the word.

She lies back on the bed, her hands rest at the hem of her gown that's risen on her parted thighs, looks to the ceiling, takes a deep breath, then looks back at me, and waits for my next command. She's so innocent and vulnerable. I'm going to make this good for her. It's all about her tonight. The thought of my lips on her pussy makes my dick swell and beg for attention, but I'm only focused on making her feel good. I want her to let go completely.

Even if for only a moment. Perhaps that's all she needs to feel this between us. The pull that is near crippling for me.

I lean forward and push the fabric up her stomach. I kiss along her belly and marvel at the silver marks barely visible on her body. I nuzzle into her belly and kiss her stretch marks. One at a time, loving how they'll stay with her. They're evidence of her strength. She writhes under me and I move lower. Kissing and nipping her soft skin.

Soft moans escape and she nearly moves her hand to my hair. That's my good girl.

I push my thumbs through the thin fabric that separates her heat from me and rip it off her, tossing it carelessly to the side of the bed. Her lips part in shock and I watch her pussy clench and glisten with arousal. Yes baby, let me please you. I lick my lips and gently lift my fingers to her heat, finding her wet. That takes me by surprise, and I fucking love it. I almost push my fingers into her tight pussy but think better of it. She said she was sore...even if she lied, I'm not going to enter her. I'll make her come on my tongue and nothing else.

I'll give, and I'll take nothing. I'll show her my worth and my desire. Maybe she'll grow to love me, even if she never feels what I feel for her. I will take anything—a morsel of affection from her could bring me to my knees.

Her breathing quickens as I lean down and take a long, languid swipe of her pussy and groan. Fuck, she tastes so damn good. A tang that makes my mouth water. My fingers dig into her hips, holding her down and open so I can get more of her on my tongue. I dip into her heat and curl my tongue to massage the front wall of her pussy. The sound of her gasping and grabbing the sheets as she writhes at my touch makes me grin into her pussy. I give her another lick before moving to her throbbing clit.

As I suckle her clit gently, listening to her soft moans, a thought strikes me. Did he ever lick her this way and give her pleasure that she should have only gotten from my touch? The image of that asshole giving her pleasure heats my blood and fuels my need to taste her arousal. I growl against her heat and ravage her pussy like a starving man. Angry at the knowledge that he ever had a taste of my mate makes me suck her harder without any mercy. My tongue flicks and massages against her clit as she screams out her orgasm and shatters beneath me. I groan with pleasure as her body trembles in my hands. Her hips attempt to buck against me, but I grip her tighter and force her ass back onto the bed.

She's going to fucking take it.

I lick up her arousal before diving into her heat with my rigid, thick tongue. I want more. Her tiny fists move to cover her mouth and muffle her screams of pleasure. Her heels dig deeper into the mattress as her body tries to move away from the intense waves of pleasure. I breathe into her heat and lick her clit as my fingers dip slightly into her tight pussy. With one arm reaching up her torso, I hold her there and cup her breast at the same time. Kneading and plucking her hardened peak. Her back arches with another moan and I love every second of her pleasure. She's soaking wet and I want so badly to enter her, even if it's only with my fingers. "You too sore for my fingers baby?" I have no fucking clue how my voice comes out smooth and confident. Teasingly almost. My breathing is uneven and labored, and I'm on the verge of begging to be inside her. But my words show no hint of my desperation.

She shakes her head, her eyes tightly closed, and moans, "Please." A grin pulls at my lips.

I can't help myself. "Please what baby?" I stare at her beautiful, flushed face and bunch the fabric farther up her body, exposing the hard peaks of her nipples. I cup her full breast before pinching her nipple between my fingers once again. She jumps at the contact, but I push her hip down with my other hand.

She moans low and sensual as her eyes slowly find mine. She looks hazy with lust as she bites her lip and blushes. "I want your fingers, please."

Fuck. Those words on her lips tempt me to fuck her. My erection bobs with need between us, leaking more precum at her softly spoken plea. I close my eyes and groan, thanking the gods for blessing me with my mate before leaning down and sucking her clit while I push two thick fingers into her dripping pussy. I moan against her clit at the feel of her tight walls pulsing against my fingers. I pull back to watch her as her back arches off the bed. She's so fucking beautiful. My thumb pushes against her clit as my fingers stroke her front wall. Her gasps of pleasure coming from her plump lips fill my chest with pride.

I bend while keeping my eyes on her and suckle her clit, pumping my fingers relentlessly into her wet core. Her moans get louder and louder as she approaches her release. Her fingers pull at my hair and scratch my scalp as she pushes my face into her greedy pussy. Her need for me makes me want to smile, but I keep finger fucking her and sucking her clit faster and harder, giving her exactly what she wants. It doesn't take long for her body to bow and for her hands to leave my head and cover her mouth as she screams in utter ecstasy.

I pull back, letting her clit pop as I lose suction on her. Her body jolts at the sensation and I stare down at her quivering body with a heated gaze. Her taste covers my mouth as I lick my lips, enjoying the sight of her and the knowledge that I made her come. I made her feel alive. Her hazel eyes travel down her body and meet my stare. A shock goes through me as her eyes brighten with lust and more. An intense pull pulses between us. Our breathing slows in unison as we stare into each other's eyes. She has to be feeling this. I need her to feel the pull that I feel to her.

Please tell me you feel it baby.

Just as I make a move to crawl up her body and give her true pleasure, the fucking baby monitor goes off with the sound of our little one crying. Red coloring fills the sound bars on the screen as the wails continue. The lustful trance between us is shattered as her eyes dart to the monitor and she pulls her legs together and into her stomach. She turns over and props herself up, ready to run to her crying infant. She stills and her breath stalls as she glances at me and then down to the floor. A look of guilt passes over her face, and I don't understand why.

Not until she opens her mouth. "I'm sorry. May I leave to get him?" Her eyes don't leave the floor as she whispers her request. My hands go numb as a cold wave washes over my body. The electricity between us dims to nothing as she shifts uncomfortably. "I'm sorry." She speaks softly with true remorse. She swallows as her eyes dart to mine after a moment of silence.

My heart is fucking shattered at her submissive posture. "There's nothing to be sorry for." My hand finds hers on the bed and squeezes. "You don't need permission." I lean across the bed and kiss her lips with a tenderness I haven't shown her yet. I need her to feel my love. To feel this. She leans into the kiss and lifts her small hand to my jaw. It hovers with a moment of hesitation before she actually touches me. My wolf rumbles with approval and brushes against my chest, wanting to feel more of her touch. But I have to pull back and let her tend to the baby who lets out another piercing wail.

CHAPTER 8

LENA

My son wriggles in my arms, waking me. My eyes slowly open and I can't help but to smile down at him. Safe and so far from a fate I worried about. Adjusting him in the crook of my arm, I hold him just right so he can eat. Hungry little wolf. It's been so long since falling asleep hasn't been met with fear of what could come in the morning. My smile slips as I feel Jude's heavy arm across my hips. He's on his side and quietly snoring. A hint of the smile returns as I peek up at his handsome face. I adjust again so I can see him better, still cradling my little one. Jude's plump lips are parted and smooshed against the pillow.

I don't know what to think of this wolf. Or what his true

intentions are. I don't even know if I can believe him, but I don't understand why he would do so much for me if he didn't truly think he was mated to me. All I know is that this child of mine isn't the only pup who needs me and needs me to make the right steps moving forward and with caution.

With the early morning light filtering in, I'm desperate to find Addy and Reese. It's early, but I'd like to be there when they wake up. Yesterday was odd with the other women. They seem very friendly, but I'm wary still. I don't know what this pack has planned for me and my family. Jude claims he's my mate and that may very well save me. My eyes fall on his massive, muscular body. Any woman would be lucky to have him as a mate. At least from what I know of him so far. But this isn't the first time I've been claimed by a wolf, and I don't know what to believe.

There is warmth when I see him and think of him, probably because of what he did last night. I've never felt such pleasure. And of course I'm grateful. I'm indebted to him.

But the pull of a mate? That doesn't exist for me.

It takes a bit of maneuvering, but I'm able to slip out from his hold while keeping my son in my arms. My stomach growls as I tiptoe out to the dresser. I quickly and quietly change his diaper, watching how his little legs kick out and then bunch back up. His eyes seem to focus on my face, but only for a moment. My heart swells with happiness in my chest. I still need to name him, but I have no idea what he should be called. I'm of the belief that names hold value and I want his name to represent strength. He's going to need it to survive this world. I bundle him up and quietly leave Jude's bedroom to search for my niece and nephew. I need to make sure they slept all right and that they've eaten. I don't truly trust anyone here.

The absolute truth of what's happened is that I don't know what to think or believe and I'm terrified of what's to come because it's out of my control.

I'm momentarily shocked as I hear Addy's laugh over the pads of my feet smacking along the wooden hall floor. I slow my steps and listen.

"So how old are you?" I think that's Grace's voice.

"Two, silly." Addy giggles again. Her little voice is full of joy.

"Two! Two!" Reece squeals and shrieks with laughter. Emotions make my throat dry and tears prick. They're laughing. It's been so long since I've heard them laugh.

My inhale stutters and I try to contain myself.

"No Reece. No!" Even on the verge of tears, I have to stifle a laugh at Addy scolding Reece. "You one." I peek my head around the corner. Wearing nothing but a diaper, Reece is seated on the tabletop playing with orange slices. He shoves one in his mouth and smiles. Lizzie puts her hands up and hides behind them before poking her head around the side and quickly hiding again. Reece shrieks with delight.

"So you're the oldest then?" Grace talks to Addy and Addy

nods her head dramatically.

Her chin nearly bounces off her chest. "Yea." She finally gets out a word before snagging one of Reece's orange slices. "Mo' please!" She holds the orange in front of Grace as though she's offering it, but quickly shoves it into her mouth and giggles at Grace's playful, offended reaction.

"I didn't get any oranges! Could I have one? Please?" Grace holds her finger up and pleads with Addy.

Reece shrieks something unrecognizable and tries to push an orange into Grace's mouth. The room fills with genuine laughter and it's nearly too much. It's hard to believe it's real, like there isn't an ulterior motive I haven't seen. Like we aren't being used. I gently pat my son's bottom and rock him in my arms to soothe him as I watch the women take care of my family. I remember what Lizzie said to calm me when my baby was coming. I remember that bond, and soothing energy overwhelms me. I'm so grateful I have the help. Tears form in my eyes. I'm overwhelmed with the intense emotions riding through me.

I want nothing more than for this to be real.

As I hear Jude's loud steps come from behind me, I still. I'd planned to go back. I didn't want to upset him again. Air freezes in my lungs, and my hands tighten on my son. I hold him close to my chest and swallow the lump growing in my throat. He won't be pleased. I should have gone back immediately.

With a deep rumble behind me, his hands wrap around my hips, and he pulls my back into his hard chest. A calming wave flows through me at his firm but loving touch. His soft lips plant a kiss on my neck and I tilt my head to offer him more. "There you are." My body involuntarily pushes into him, and I arch my back, nuzzling my ass into him. My eyes widen. I have no idea why I did that. Or why my body heats from head to toe at the feel of him hardening against my ass. I'm gifted a rumble of approval that vibrates through his hard chest as he kisses my hair and runs his fingers along the sides of my stomach.

It feels...different.

"Did you just get up?" His question reminds me of my disobedience; I stiffen slightly and part my lips to apologize, but he interrupts me. "I want to make pancakes for the kiddos. They can eat pancakes right?"

My shoulders relax as I chance a look at him, peeking over my shoulder. His eyes shine with devotion and love as I nod. "They haven't had them before, but they can eat them." He grins and kisses my cheek before leaving me and heading toward the kitchen. He glances over his shoulder. "You want some too, baby? You've got to be hungry after last night." He smirks at me as he walks ahead and that feeling comes back. Just an ounce of it...of something I haven't felt before.

CHAPTER 9

JUDE

S he's denied me but I think she's coming around. I'll show her what being a true mate means. She's jaded from the shit Shadow put her through. At least that's what I've gathered from the little bits and pieces she's told me over the last few hours. She's kept to her word, giving me little bits of what happened to help me understand and letting me ask questions. She's jaded from more than just Shadow... there're also the fucking seers.

Seers keep screwing me over. First they play my father against me and my brothers. And now my mate has yet another reason to question my claim to her all because of something a seer once told her. The seers are wrong. I've no intention of going back to my father's pack and never will. Life is good with Devin. I trust him to make the right decisions, so I don't have to worry about anything other than my mate and her happiness. I glance at Lena, grateful to be outside under the warmth of the afternoon sun. This morning has been easy going so far, little conversations kept light, and small moments where I swear she must feel something.

I watch Lena swing little Reece in her arms as he giggles. I glance between them and our little one who's fighting sleep in Lizzie's arms.

Lena was hesitant to let Lizzie hold our little boy, but I'm glad she allowed it. I want to see Lena's wolf. My own is dying to get out and run with her. Grace and Lizzie sit next to each other in the grass cooing at the little boy.

I squat in front of Addy to get down to her level. "Does your wolf want to come out?"

"Woof! Woof!" Addy and Reece start barking and chasing each other. I'm not sure if they understood, but they'll get the picture when I shift. I smile at my mate. "Let's go for a run." She nods reluctantly and looks back at Lizzie and Grace.

"We'll stay with the kids," Grace says, and I swear Lizzie must say something too because she shares a look with Lena. It's a moment that lasts a bit too long with a flash of emotion from Lena that's quickly eased. I can't help but feel a pang of jealousy that Lizzie's bonded with her, Lena can hear her, and I can't. Swallowing thickly, I focus on the gratitude that she has someone to ease her worries. Finally, as I calm the growing tide of emotion, Lena stands, heads to the edge of the woods for privacy with me and slips off her dress.

I'm mesmerized as she stretches catlike and smoothly transitions into her wolf. Shades of tan and white meld together in her fur and call to me to rub against it. Before I'm even aware, my wolf takes over. His desperation outweighs my consciousness. Perhaps aided by the pull of the moon coming. I shift and run to be by her side. Feeling the sweet stretch of release. My wolf rubs his side against hers and playfully nuzzles into her neck. Her wolf responds with caution. Lowering herself to the ground. I pace around her, waiting for her to rise. She doesn't and my wolf doesn't understand; he whimpers, nudging her.

At the sound of a small gasp, I look up to see Reece and Addy staring wide-eyed and stiff as boards watching us. I don't understand their reaction, but my wolf smells their fear. For a moment, I question allowing my wolf to stay seen. I know I'm a rather large wolf and that could be intimidating, but still their fear is unwarranted. My wolf lays panting on the ground with his tongue out. Looking between our mate and the younglings. He barks once wanting someone to interact with him without fear. But all the bark does is jolt the children. Our mate responds by rolling to her side and exposing her belly.

At the sight my blood runs cold. She's afraid. Her wolf is

terrified and so are the children. And I have no idea why. I urge my wolf to crawl to her, so he doesn't upset her, and lick her neck. She stills at the contact before relaxing. He nuzzles into her again and then rises and jumps playfully over her and nudges her to play. He wants to run with his mate. The pain that radiates through me, from him, is chilling. As much as Lena is my mate, her wolf is his and something's happened. He doesn't understand and he whimpers again. I don't blame him. I want to see her run as well. She's strong and healthy. She's stunning, but her fear detracts from the beauty.

She slowly rises, keeping her head lowered and my wolf nudges under her chin and pounces playfully at her. She finally barks back. From the corner of my eye I see the children quietly approaching. This morning I gently prodded for Lena to tell me little bits and pieces, but I never asked about her wolf. I never asked about the children's wolves either. My heart beats slowly, realizing perhaps I should have. I can smell their fear, but I'm happy they have the courage to approach. Is it possible they've never seen someone shift? I can't imagine that's the case. I turn to them and little Reece steps back and trips over his own feet, landing on his butt. My wolf chortles and slowly paces to him before lying beside him so he can pet me.

At first, the children still with fear. But my wolf is patient. Content to be around children. Around family. The thought makes my heart clench. It's been too long since I've seen my brothers. And now that I know they have a mate, I long to see them even more. After a moment Reece and Addy pet my wolf and my mate lays beside me. My wolf wants to run, but he's content just lying lazily so long as our mate and the children are happy. Addy squeals with a mix of delight and disgust as my wolf licks her face, leaving a trail of slobber behind. Reece claps his little hands and yells, "Mo! Mo!" More. His happiness fuels my wolf to scoot forward and give him a slobbery kiss. He shrieks with joy as he pushes me away.

It's an odd feeling, allowing my wolf to take over and not having complete control, not being able to communicate with Lena and only watching. I wish nothing more than for her to hear me. Baby? I attempt but she doesn't respond, and her wolf doesn't seem to notice either.

A noise to my left distracts me. In the distance, Vince and Devin talk on the steps of the house. As I catch Devin's eyes, he motions for me to join them. My wolf is reluctant, but I push him to move, and I give my mate one more nuzzle before rising and galloping toward the steps. Without breaking my stride, I shift. I'm left feeling uncertain and have far too many questions as I obey my Alpha and leave Lena and the children in the field.

"Alpha?" Devin looks pissed. He's usually fairly intense and has a look about him that warns people to stay away, but over the years I've learned the subtle hints of his emotions. And right now, he's truly pissed. I can't help but to worry that it has something to do with Lena until he speaks.

"Fucking vampires." I look to Vince expecting him to flinch from Devin's response. I'm shocked that he doesn't, considering his mate is a vampire.

"What happened?" I ask.

Vince only huffs, sitting with his legs wider on the steps of the porch. Both of them wear blue jeans, with Devin wearing a collared shirt and Vince wearing a white tee that stretches across his broad shoulders. "Veronica's queen is getting pushback from other covens. A faction is growing and they want her support."

"Support for what?" I join them, sitting on the steps and watching my mate prance around while the children chase her. Even with the pleasing sight, nerves rattle their way through me.

"They're revolting against the Authority. More than just the vampires."

"Everyone's fed up with the corruption," Vince speaks with distaste. "The threats and laws about blood and feeding..." Vince cracks his neck and looks back at the house. No doubt thinking of his mate.

Devin gets to the point. "An internal war has started among the vampires. Veronica's coven wants protection."

"It should be easy enough since they're close." I answer knowing I'll need more information but fairly certain it won't be much of a challenge. Vince doesn't look convinced, and a chill runs down my spine. "What kind of war are we talking about?"

"A cold one currently. Only spoken threats. Each is counting their numbers and gathering alliances. The division is growing." Vince gives Devin a hard look that gets my attention.

"Jude, there's something you should know." My body stills at Devin's tone. I don't fucking like it.

"Your father's pack is going against the Authority. They've made their loyalty to the vampires known."

My blood turns to ice. That's a stupid decision to make. My father's a fool. Even knowing he'd planned to have my brothers and me killed, I hurt for him and his pack. His decision to rise against the Authority will cost them. The words from the woman in Alec's office ring in my head. That I should go see my brothers. My hand runs along my jaw as I let my emotions settle.

"If there's anyone at all in your old pack that you want spared, now is the time to reach out to them. We will offer them protection." I nod, acknowledging my Alpha. I remember nearly all of my old pack. The only one I hold ill will toward is my father. My jaw clenches as my wolf growls with anger. My mate's eyes fly to mine as she stills in shock and lowers herself. I silently scold my wolf for startling her and rise to go to her.

"Any news of my brothers?" I have to ask before I go to her, hating that we aren't bonded so she can't hear me. It would kill me to know that they're siding against the Authority.

"Not that we've heard." Vince answers as Veronica walks to him. Her long black dress blows easily in the afternoon wind. I nod to her as she approaches, and she does the same to me.

I tell them both, "I'll reach out to my brothers and decide what to do."

The moment Devin nods with approval, I make my way back to my mate. In my heart, I already know I'll have to go to them. I have to offer my old pack protection against my father's unwise decision. But the thought of facing him chills me to the core.

It's unsettling. So much of the day is unsettling, although there's so much to be thankful for.

Lena shifts into human form and immediately bows as I approach her. The children stay still and go quiet. It's more than obvious she's still startled and they're cautious as well. I offer them a smile and without hesitation sit in front of my mate cupping her chin and kissing her sweet lips as soon as she raises her head. Tension breaks in an instant and her body relaxes.

I hate her submission and her fear of me. I'm determined to break it.

"I saw you were angry." Her eyes stay on my lips as she speaks. I wish she'd look me in the eyes. I stay on the ground in front of her and kiss her again. I revel in the fact that she kisses me back and relaxes in my embrace.

"Nothing you need to worry about, baby." I smile again at her niece and nephew, and they smile back with toothy grins. It only takes a prod from Lizzie and Grace to play chase and Addy yells out a squeal and starts barking and running. Reece attempts to chase her but trips over his little legs. He squeals and gets up quickly to follow his big sister.

I grin at them and watch as Addy runs circles around Reece. "You'd think he'd shift so he could keep up."

"We weren't permitted to shift." Lena looks uncomfortable as she speaks, and as much as I'm shocked, I'm grateful for her admission. My teeth bite down hard, and I struggle to relax. It takes everything in me to contain my anger.

"Do they know how?" I can't believe he'd hurt their wolves like that. At least they're young so the damage will be minimal.

"Addy did once." Her words are soft and coated in sadness. I rein in my anger once again before wrapping an arm around her and pulling her between my legs. She turns her body to face the children but looks over my shoulder at Lizzie and Grace. Devin's whispering in Grace's ear and making her blush. It's not hard to guess that he's bribing her with a baby of her own as she passes the little boy to Lizzie. I can see Lena's fingers twitch to hold her baby.

"I think she might keep him if you don't go get him." I whisper, teasing her. A quick flash of fear crosses her faces before she shakes her head, and the hint of a smile shows on her face. She rises, but keeps her eyes on me, as if she expects me to stop her. I kiss her thigh as she reaches for her dress, slipping it on easily. Lizzie sees Lena approaching and mocks a pout before giving the baby a quick kiss on the forehead. She smiles brightly as she holds the little boy up for Lena.

Listening to the children play and watching my mate cuddle our baby makes me yearn for an even bigger family. It reminds me that I've yet to claim my mate. The full moon will be here soon, and I want to make sure she knows I intend to claim her. That bastard mark from Shadow will be ruined as soon as I get a chance to scar over it.

She settles beside me and raises the wiggly baby to her breast. "Just in time." She sighs happily as he latches.

"I want to claim you on the full moon." I'm almost ashamed of how blunt I am. Her smile falls.

She seems scared to speak but finally she answers. "I don't want that."

Shocked by her statement, a crushing weight comes down over me. I lean forward in the grass to get closer to her, to ask why and to try to understand, and I immediately curse myself as she hunches her shoulders. As if she's preparing for a blow. I slowly put my arm around her and kiss her shoulder.

Although I'm saddened by her admission, I'm grateful she's at least being honest and no longer censoring herself. I need to find out why though. I need to destroy whatever is standing in her way of accepting me. I don't know what would become of me if I cannot claim my mate.

"Does it matter that much that I'm not an Alpha? Are you ashamed of me?" I know the seers promised her an Alpha as a mate. My chest pains with the thought that she doesn't see me as a worthy mate.

She stares back at me as she rocks the little one who is quietly eating. "You're not the first to tell me I'm your mate."

"He had no right." I check my anger and calm myself. That bastard is dead. There's nothing more I can do regarding him and I refuse to speak his name. "Don't you feel a pull to me," I whisper, "even just a little?" I remember the moment we had in the bedroom and pray she felt it too. I wait with bated breath as her hazel eyes find mine. She nestles into my side and sighs. I love the contact and so does my wolf.

"Yes." She barely whispers with her eyes closed. My heart soars in my chest. A weight lifts off my shoulders and I feel my lips pull into a grin, but it's quick to fall.

"Then why won't you let me claim you?" If she feels the pull than it will only get stronger as the moon approaches.

"I'm scared," she answers in a hushed voice, staring at the ground rather than at me.

I can't help but to push for more. "Why are you so afraid? I won't treat you like Shadow did. You have to know that."

She shakes her head. "You've already treated me with more kindness than he ever did."

"Then why don't you want me to claim you?"

"The burn." Her hand not holding her baby rises to the mark on her neck as tears well in her eyes.

I've heard it can hurt. I've also heard it's nothing but pleasure. All I know is that it must happen for our bond to be complete. "I promise I won't hurt you as your mate."

Although she nods and seems to agree, I can see it in her eyes that she doesn't want to be claimed. She doesn't trust that I won't let her suffer the pain on her own. A deep hurt settles in my chest.

"Think about it?" I ask her. "For me."

She stares back at me, as if seeing through me, before promising, "I will."

CHAPTER 10

JUDE

"We were just talking about you." I smile into the phone as Luke answers the ring. I lean my back against the wall in the dimly lit living room. There's enough light from the large windows that I don't bother switching on a ceiling light. I haven't sat down either. I turn and lean against the window frame reminding myself it's just a phone call. It's been far too long since I've heard my brother's voice though. The timbre of his tone brings back memories from when we were only children.

"And why would you two be talking about me?" It makes me happy to know they haven't forgotten me. At times I miss my brothers, but it's best we chose different packs. I often remind myself of that.

There's a pause before he answers. "It's something we'd rather discuss in person." I tense, not liking a damn thing about that response. The conversation that needs to happen. I'm not waiting when his tone holds too much concern. I know I'll fixate on it; I'll think the worst and with everything happening, so many parts moving at once, I can't allow that to happen.

"Is Owen there?" I question.

"Yeah, we're both here."

"Put it on speaker. I want to get this out and over with." I pace the front of the room and watch as my mate shifts for the children. Lizzie's watching and I can see she's trying her damndest to shift. It's disheartening, but it will happen. The entire pack has faith.

"One second," he says and then there's a muffling on the phone.

With a resigned sigh, I step away from the window. I hear Luke pull the phone away from his ear and set it on a table or something that makes a clanging noise into the phone.

"Sweetness, go get us lunch." I smirk as Owen gives an order, although barely audible on my end, to presumably his mate. Their mate. "You could at least ask nicely." Her soft voice is followed by the sound of her kissing someone and then a "please" from one of my brothers. I'm not sure which gets the next kiss and then there's a chuckle and a loud smack.

I assume a palm to her ass.

The seriousness of the conversation is dimmed by the interaction, and I find myself looking back out the window at my Lena.

"What's going on big bro?" Owen speaks first as I hear the phone shift slightly on their end.

"I take it you two are doing well with your mate."

"You've got to meet her Jude." I don't even try to repress my smile at his lovesick tone.

"Soon. Very soon in fact." I swallow and pinch the bridge of my nose. "Have either of you spoken to our father recently?"

"Fuck no." Luke's hard words are exactly what I expected to hear.

I hesitate to ask, but it must be done, "Have you heard any whispers of war?"

"Yes." Owen is quick to respond. My brow rises up my forehead and I still. I wasn't expecting them to have heard anything about it.

"Our father has apparently made his position in the war known. He's planning to side with the vampires." I shake my head, not liking that I've grouped all of the vampires together. "The ones going against the Authority." Silence on their end makes me weary. "Don't tell me you've sided against the Authority." My breath leaves me at their lack of an immediate answer.

"All right, Jude." I've always liked Luke's no-nonsense attitude. "Here's what we know. We've got a coven that wants protection. We promised them safety against the other vamps. We're on the side of the Authority. We don't know shit about our old pack." After a moment he adds, "That's fucked." I finally breathe and find myself tapping against the window frame. They're in the same position as my pack. Good.

"Thank fuck." I relax my shoulders and roll them to get rid of the tension. "You had me worried there."

"It's not all vamps. Emma's been doing research for the Authority."

I cut him off. "Owen, I know. I know. We're protecting a coven also. The faction is growing and sides have mostly been chosen."

"I can't believe our father is on the other side."

A snort from Luke interrupts Owen. "I can. I just feel sorry for our pack. Our old pack."

"I feel you on that. I'm not all right with his decision. I can't stand by and watch it happen." Tension coils in my muscles as I prepare to ask them for something I never thought I would. "Luke. Owen. We need to meet." And now for the part I've been dreading. "I think we should go to Gray Mountain." The silence on the other end of the phone tells me of their hesitancy.

"The last time we were there—"

I cut Owen off. "That was years ago."

"It doesn't change the fact."

"You're right. Nothing will ever change the fact that our

father was planning to kill us. I know that."

"I don't want to see him, Jude." Luke's voice is hard, but I know why. I know it's the pain from our father abandoning and hating us. I know he's hurt more than anything else.

"What if he sees this as a threat Jude? He could view us coming to him as the seer's vision coming true." Owen's always been logical. I hadn't really considered that.

"What if we don't go? Would you be able to rest well knowing he led them to war? A war against the Authority." My heart twists and sinks in my hollow chest. "A war against us."

"He wouldn't." Even before Owen finishes speaking, the conviction is gone from his voice.

"He would."

Luke speaks to Owen, "You know he would. He'd lead his pack to war against us."

"We need to convince him otherwise." My gaze finds my mate as I pace back to the window. "I want to avoid this war." I watch her chase the little ones around in the grass.

"After all, it's only our father that we have to convince. Only him who betrayed us. We know everyone else, and what the Betas did to protect us." They risked their lives to get us away from him. They protected us against their own Alpha. "We owe them. We can't let our father lead them to death."

"And what happens if he refuses?" Owen has a good point. I sigh heavily, not knowing the answer.

"All we can do is try." After a long moment of silence, they finally agree.

"We'll meet you at Gray Mountain."

"We'll be there at sunrise."

As I stare out the window, watching my pack, I swallow thickly and respond, "I'll tell my Alpha and we'll meet you there."

THE SIGHT OF US MUST BE INTIMIDATING, I almost regret bringing everyone. But hopefully, together, we'll be able to sway our father and prevent his alliance with the vampires. Without our mates, our presence would be seen as a challenge. Devin suggested and I reluctantly agreed, our mates will accompany us and aid us in the endeavor to sway him. Lena walks hesitantly behind me, our son tucked away peacefully with his head against her chest. Emma, my brothers' mate, who's on the shorter side, and Grace walk with her. Our mates are shielded by Devin on my left and my brothers on my right. Behind them are Vince, Veronica, and Lev. Veronica seems a bit off, less vocal and sharp than usual and Vince is tending to her much more than he has before. I nearly objected to them coming, but it's not my call to make.

I recognize the guard on duty, running his laps around the estate. Daniel. He's grown to be quite a large shifter since I've last seen him. He's a few years younger than me, but we occasionally played together, and he took his sparring lessons with my brothers. He's a good wolf. Genuinely caring and eager to help others. A sadness swells in my chest as memories of my childhood flash before my eyes. The estate looks the same as it did back then. Log cabins littered among ancient trees with a lake house in the center for all to commune. Even with the bite of the chill today, the sun shines down through the sparse trees and offers warmth. I was blessed with happiness and a righteous pack. But all that changed years ago.

Daniel stops when he sees us and squares his shoulders before he recognizes me. As our eyes meet, a smile brightens his face and he strides toward us with his arms out. He's roughly my height, wearing worn jeans just as my brothers and I are. A touch of nostalgia brings me back. I embrace him quickly and pat his back with a force that would have a weaker wolf stumbling. A rough laugh bellows from his chest as he takes in my brothers.

"Long time no see, Jude. Luke. Owen." He nods to each of us before seeing the rest of us. His smile dims. "Is everything all right?" The light in his eyes dulls as Devin introduces himself and the rest of the pack, and we tell him we're here to see our father to discuss the matters of the Authority. He nods solemnly until I introduce Lena, stepping aside and allowing her to come to my side. She does so naturally, and I wrap my arm around her waist, not too tight or possessive, just enough so that she knows she's safe.

"It's nice to meet you," she answers and takes a peek over her shoulder toward Grace, who steps up as Devin continues the introductions. Lena doesn't move as I half expect her to, in fact, she leans into me just slightly. "We'll be back tonight," I promise her.

She nods, closing her parted lips and staring straight ahead. There's something there, but before it can take hold, Daniel leads us to my father. The walk to the larger log cabin where the Alpha resides is nearly silent and bathed with anxious tension.

It's obvious Daniel has questions, but he's biting his tongue. Lena as well, who walks beside me, her hand in mine. I can only imagine what she's thinking.

As we near the stairs Daniel finally speaks, "You know, we weren't sure what came of you three." My brows raise in surprise.

Luke laughs. "You thought he got us, Daniel?" He playfully slaps Daniel on his back.

"I'm being serious." Daniel's saddened tone doesn't wane with Luke's playfulness. "We thought something happened when no one had seen any of you for days."

"No one told you what happened?" I question and although Daniel looks back at me, it's Lena's eyes on me that I feel.

"Told us what?" It's then that I realize the Betas mustn't have said anything about helping us escape. The seer's vision was common knowledge as was our father's reaction to the casting.

"Nothing." I shake my head. "We're sorry Daniel. If we'd known we were leaving I'd have spread word. Everything happened quickly." I breathe deeply, remembering the tension and anxiety I felt as a boy. My wolf stirs restlessly, not liking the memory.

At his movement, Lena looks up at me and I know her wolf must've sensed it too. I speak in my head, only calling her name, but she doesn't respond. With Devin's curious glance, I turn back to Daniel.

"Don't apologize. I'm just happy to see you three." He gives us a semblance of a smile. "Are you staying long?" The way he asks the question and the look in his eyes makes me think he's asking more. Asking if we've come back to reclaim the pack. I don't want him to think that. I don't want anyone to think we've come to challenge our father. His eyes dart to our mates and then back to me as he presses his lips into a hard line. I smile knowing he doesn't approve of us bringing the women if we've come to fight. He's a good man.

"We're only here to talk alliances." Devin answers for me.

"Ah. For the war," he says far too easily.

I nod and continue searching his face. He doesn't give any hint of his opinion on the matter.

"And what do you think of this war?" Devin questions. He's a bit overdressed in my opinion. Suit pants and a button down with no tie. His sleeves are rolled up at least. Daniel shifts his weight uncomfortably.

"It's not my place to say. I'm not the Alpha."

"I'm just curious to know your opinion is all." I forgot how my father ran his pack. He takes his dictatorship seriously. I confide in Daniel, "We came to convince him not to go against the Authority." His eyes brighten with hope and his shoulders lift with optimism before quickly dropping.

He swallows and looks to his left and right before answering. No one is around to see us. I imagine the pack is just rising given the early morning. It's far too early for anyone else to be spectating and that's exactly how I wanted this to happen. I didn't want it to be a show.

"I'm not sure he'll agree." He looks over his shoulder again and licks his lips with nervousness. "But it would make many of us happy if you were to convince him."

"How many?" I remember when I was younger we weren't to discuss pack matters. Not a word was to be said in question of the Alpha's decisions. My father was a true dictator. He was kind and righteous, or was until that fateful day, so no one sought to disagree with him. Ever. The fact that Daniel speaks for "many" means times have changed.

I glance behind him at the small cottages that are scattered on the property. The larger log cabin is in the center. It holds the Betas and the Alpha's family. Or it used to. The wood has been recently washed and the cottages are well kept. The large farm and market that we passed on the way was brimming with produce and the livestock was obviously well fed. The pack is thriving, which is good to see. But if there have been whispers from the pack that go against my father's decision, then the pack is not as strong as it should be.

"I'd rather not say, Jude." I nod my head and respect his decision to remain quiet.

"I understand." I pat him on the back in thanks and start to make my way to the large, carved wooden doors, but his hand grabs my arm, stopping me from leaving.

His eyes plead with me and his voice speaks of urgency. "We would be happy if you stayed." His eyes dart to my brothers before he quickly leaves us on the steps to my father's cabin.

"Do we have to go in?" My brothers' mate asks warily from behind me as she tugs on Owen's and Luke's arms. In a casual dress that flows to her knees and a cardigan, their mate would appear carefree, if not for the concern clearly written on her face.

According to my brothers, she knows more than most, but she's been just as quiet and reserved as Lena.

"If you want to stay here, you can." She shakes her head nearly violently at Luke's response.

"No, I don't want us to go in." She looks at the rest of us with fear in her eyes. She's right to be afraid, but my brothers won't let anything happen to her.

"We have to do this, Emma."

"I have a bad feeling, Luke." Her voice chokes and her words come out strangled as her eyes widen. Lena holds my hand tighter.

"It's all right." Owen kisses her forehead. "Nothing's going to happen to us."

Luke gives her waist a small squeeze before leaning down to kiss his mark. "It'll be fine. In and out, just stay beside us."

I half expect my adrenaline to surge, or for any anxiousness at all to wreak havoc on my conscious. But I feel nothing but calm determination. After sharing a look with Devin, I assure all of them, "We will do what we came to do and then leave."

Grace nods in agreement.

"That's my mate." He playfully nips her ear lobe and smiles. "We'll be home soon."

I turn and give my own mate a kiss. "Stay behind me, all right baby?" I kiss our son's little head poking out from fabric she's got wrapped around her and tied to hold him to her chest.

"Of course." She nods and runs soothing circles on the little boy's back. She appears more confident than Emma, but I can sense a hint of worry. I give her a reassuring smile and lead the way. I glance at Grace as I open the doors and she looks like she gives about the same number of fucks as Devin does. Which would be zero. Although there's a small uneasy feeling in my gut, I know we'll be fine. We aren't breaking any pack laws. There's no reason to worry. We'll speak with him, if he'll allow it, and leave.

As we enter the cabin, I'm flooded with memories. The dark wooden floors shine and appear pristine, but I know in the hall on the second floor, by my old room, there's a gouge in one of the planks from where I attempted to carve my name in the floor. I smile sadly as I lead us down the large hall to the meeting room. My heartbeat gets louder as blood rushes in my ears. I'm certain Daniel has made my father aware that we're here. It depresses me that I can no longer hear their thoughts. When we left and broke the bond to our father, we gave up the bond to the entire pack. A pain rips through my chest as I near the back room and find Leon and Marcellus standing by the doors. The Betas. I owe them my life. As do my brothers.

I push the bastard emotions growing in my chest down. As the restlessness creeps down my spine, Lena squeezes my hand.

Both Betas offer a tight smile and nod slightly, no doubt concerned for the meeting. I nod in turn and wait while they open the doors and allow us entry. They don't speak, although when they catch sight of our mates, a sense of ease appears and I'm grateful for it. I need a moment to keep my composure from breaking. I thought I'd long dealt with the sadness from leaving my pack and the pain of betrayal from my father. I harden my heart and walk with determination to the head of the long table in the center of the room. Devin's hand comes down hard on my shoulder and he squeezes slightly as he passes me to sit on my left. He places Grace next to him. Veronica sits next to her with ease. She possesses the power and fierceness that constantly surround her, but she's paler than usual. I can't help but to think something is off as Vince places a kiss on her cheek and sits next to her. With his hand up on the table, she places hers in his. My brothers sit next to my mate at my right, Emma between the two of them. With my pack at my left and my mate and brothers at my right, I stare down the long wooden table.

Marcellus and Leon walk to the far side of the room and stand on either side of my father as he enters. Wrinkles have deepened around his eyes and his hair, cropped to his ears and brushed back, has all but grayed. The room chills as his hard, dark eyes meet mine. My fists clench as he takes the seat opposite me. The feeling of betrayal is no longer bathed in sadness and remorse for what happened years ago. Anger flares deep inside of me as I stare back at him. I'm shocked at the unwanted emotion. My wolf snarls inside my chest and all my pack is aware.

"This stays calm," Devin assures the pack in our heads, and I covertly nod, turning toward Devin in a way that introduces the two as the Alphas. Looking away, I find Lena's gaze that is riddled with questions. Both of her hands are wrapped around our little one as she sways slightly.

"Are you sure you want to lead?" Devin questions me internally and I answer that I'm fine and that I do. "I'm his eldest son, I'm the reason we're all here. I will do what I know is right."

With a deep breath, I let go of the anger. When I look back at Leon, as he introduces my father to Devin and the pack, the memory flashes before my eyes of him carrying my brothers through the field to safety, off our territory and away from our father. Leon's hair has grayed since then and his skin had dulled with wrinkles around his eyes, just like my father. I look to Marcellus and remember his hushed words as he led me to the edge of the forest. I remember his kindness and how he gave me everything I'd need to survive on my own. I cling to the memories and the fact that they're here with us now.

I clear my throat and make a determined effort to keep this short and civil as I'd planned. "Father."

"Jude." His dark eyes travel to each of us. They stop at my brothers. "Owen and Luke."

They nod their heads, but neither of them speak. I can feel the hurt radiating from each of them. Their mate grips their hands in her own and rubs her thumbs to soothe them.

"I'm surprised you brought your mates." My father's words don't get the attention of either Emma or Lena. Emma sits upright between her mates and makes no indication that she's heard, but judging by how hard she squeezes my brother's hand under the table, she certainly has. Lena is busy bouncing her little wolf in the baby carrier and kissing the top of his head. Her eyes raise to my father, and she smiles slightly before returning to care for our son. It warms my heart.

Grace clears her throat to speak, but Devin gives her a hard look and narrows his eyes, warning her to be quiet. She stares back at him with a hint of defiance before settling her back against the chair and placing her clasped hands on the table in surrender. It makes me smirk. She's so feisty for a human. When her eyes leave Devin's, an asymmetric grin appears on his face, but it's gone before he turns his attention back to the rest of us.

I give my father a false smile. "We wanted to ensure you that we come only to speak of alliances." I place both my forearms on the table with my palms down. It's not a sign of submission, but it's a sign that I'm not threatening his authority.

My father scoffs at me. Leon and Marcellus stare straight ahead, not showing any emotion. It's what my father expects from his Betas. And they've been trained well.

"I see. So you would like a section of the territory as well?" My father's tone lightens as a wicked smirk forms on his lips.

My forehead pinches in confusion. "I'm not sure I know what you're referring to."

Anger flashes in his eyes. "Well what have they offered you if not territory?"

"We haven't received any offers."

"You won't be getting one from me." His fingers strum on the table as he glances at Luke and Owen and then back at me. "I'd prefer it if we kept our distance."

"We didn't come for an offer. As I said, we'd like to form an alliance."

"You'll have to forgive me Jude, but I'd rather not be fighting alongside any of you when the war starts. We'll fight separately as much as Victor allows."

I cock a brow and comment, "I'm not sure who Victor is or why he would be dictating your pack." That pisses my father off and I quickly continue, ignoring his anger. "But if you chose to go against the Authority than you're choosing to fight against us, not with us." A maddening rage overwhelms my father as he snarls and bangs his large, clenched fists on the table. The contact makes the table shake from his anger, but my forearms remain still. I've seen his temper before and I know not reacting is the best form of defense.

Devin tenses and Veronica's back straightens. Everyone watches, keeping as still as can be.

"If you're not aligned with Victor than you're my enemy!" His eyes spark with a boiling temper as he screams across the table, spit flying from his mouth. His instant rage takes Devin back. We have the numbers, and this is only a discussion. Something in which my father has clearly lacked practice.

"Who's Victor? I haven't heard of this vampire." I keep my voice calm and even. His temper can be placated. More than that, I want to gather as much information as I can from him and pissing him off isn't necessarily the best way to accomplish that.

He's the leader of the rebellion against the Authority. He seethes and sneers as he speaks. "He's no vampire. He's a sorcerer who has seen the corruption of our politics, and he's going to give the supernaturals the territory they deserve." An ugly grimace forms on his face.

"Is that what this is about? Trading an army of shifters for more land?" It's difficult to rein in my temper, but I manage to keep the disgust from my voice. Just barely.

"It's not about the land." His large nostrils flare as he speaks. Marcellus's composure cracks as he slowly clenches his fists. My eyes fly to his, but he's focused on the back wall. Attempting to stay out of the conversation. "It's about the fact that the humans are given far too much! They should be working for the shifters and other supernaturals." His fists bang on the table once again. "It makes no sense that they are kept separate and given so much freedom. They're weak, and yet they have more than we do!" His head jerks violently to the left and his chest seems to spasm before he gains control again. He sits back in the chair breathing heavily.

"I don't find this pack to be lacking. It seems as though you have more than enough." The word "greed" lingers on my lips, but I bite my tongue.

"They're humans, weak and undeserving of equality." Shock and rage boil in my gut. I don't miss Grace's anger or how Devin's posture has changed. My father may have been a stern ruler, but I have no memory of him being so arrogant, greedy, and prejudiced. This isn't going as I thought it would. Pausing to gather temperance, I watch Leon clench his jaw to the point of nearly cracking something. He holds back his rage, and it gives me the courage to speak back against my father.

"My Alpha mate is human." Questioning his decision will most likely have us escorted out immediately, but at this point, I'm sure there will be no swaying his decision.

"That's a shame." His eyes land on Grace, who's barely containing herself. "Your Alpha must be weak." Devin only smirks in response to my father's word. Grace parts her lips although her protest is short lived.

He grips Grace's chin in his hand and kisses her to keep the words from flying out of her mouth. He doesn't seem to give a shit about my father's opinion and the fact that he easily turns his back to my father has shown him that Devin doesn't see him as a threat in the least. She's still fuming, but as he pulls back he taps his finger against her lips.

All the while my father watches and the room is filled with tense silence.

"End this now, Jude," Devin orders silently.

I prepare to make a final plea, at least one, before this gets too far out of hand and we're forced to leave.

"If you go against the Authority you will die." My voice breaks at the end and I curse the fucking emotions that erupt from me. How could I possibly feel anything but hate for this man?

"A small group of vampires almost took out the entire Authority." He sits back with an arrogant smile. "If not for the werewolves, the witches and sorcerers would have been slaughtered. What right do they have to lead us?" He laughs a cold, wicked sound. His eyes fade in and out and I question his sanity. It's as though his mind has been poisoned. "Without the shifters to aid them, the vampires won't be able to take on the Authority. I'll lead them and get rid of the undeserving Authority and Victor will reward all those who fight for the better of our species."

"The Authority has kept murder at an all-time low. Both for humans and supernaturals alike." Emma speaks hesitantly with a shaky voice. Her eyes remain on the table, and she grips her mates' hands tightly in her own. I'm surprised she spoke at all; she's so damn emotional. It's clear that she is aware of far more than I previously thought.

My father snorts, looking with disgust at the two human women in the room. My Alpha mate. My brothers' mate. How dare he behave in such a disrespectful way.

"What has become of you?" I question without thinking and his narrowed eyes meet mine.

"If only you hadn't run away, maybe you would know what this pack has been through."

"This pack's survival is why we're here," I barely murmur, emotions stirring as the memories come back again.

He seems to contemplate my statement before nearly

whispering, "Sacrifices will be made."

My fists finally clench as my anger gets the better of me. My breathing feels strained and heavy. My voice raises as I growl, "You cannot lead this pack to their death!"

With my anger, he rises, his chair scraping against the floor and nearly falling as he does. "They will go where I lead them. You gave up the right to question me when you left!" He stands at the foot of the table, and I can see the question on his face. I could challenge him for the right to this pack. I could fight him to the death to protect the people I once loved. My eyes narrow and my nostrils flare. I watch Leon and Marcellus both look at me, pleading with me.

A chill runs through my blood as Devin's warning echoes in my head but I can barely hear it.

I can't sit back and do nothing. I won't let my father destroy this pack and so many people I once loved. I'm not a child anymore. I have to do what's right.

As I realize what must be done, I see my mate, my sweet, innocent mate, shake her head. I see her chest rising and falling as she struggles for her breath. I feel her fear, but I can't stop the words from leaving my lips. "I challenge you."

My mate's loud cry resonates in my ears as my father yells, "Seize him!"

CHAPTER 11

LENA

My body is frozen in disbelief. No. I've only just met him. It's only been days that I've had with my true mate. My true mate. I could see it all play out before it happened. The moment I felt Devin's warning, when I saw the pain in my mate's eyes as the Betas stared straight at him. It was undeniable and too late to stop it. My thought shocks me and I breathe in the heavy air. It's only then that I realize I was screaming and that my poor pup is crying in my arms. I quickly hunch over him and hold him tight. I bounce slightly and try to still my trembling body. My mate has just challenged his father.

My heart falls as I slowly close my eyes. The tears tangle

with my thick lashes before falling down my face. My heart feels as though it's stopped beating. My wolf howls in agony.

Although the Betas were given orders, they hesitate, and the room is hushed in apprehension. I can barely breathe. The seers... I thought they were wrong.

"You know what the seers told you." Jude's hard words make me open my eyes. "You can back down. You can submit to me, and I will let you live."

I stare up at Jude, the cords in his neck tightening. What is he talking about? What did the seers tell him? I don't know if my mate will win. But the thought of him being in any danger causes me physical pain. I couldn't bear to let him come into danger. Something about being here has stirred a need inside of me. To protect him. To love him. My wretched, shattered heart beats wildly against my rib cage. He must be my mate. My heart twists with an aching need. And now, I may lose him forever. A strangled sob racks through my body, but I keep my lips pressed tight and continue shushing my little one. He's barely calmed.

"The seer was wrong." Jude's father raises his voice. "Victor has shown me the truth." He leans across the table and sneers. "The seer has been punished." My blood turns to ice as the air around him turns foul and his eyes flash with madness.

"Father," one of Jude's brothers says quietly, interrupting the darkest of moments. "I think you need to see a healer." I can feel the air grow tight with tension and worry as the Betas at the back of the room shift their weight.

"I don't need to listen to you! You know nothing." The Alpha snarls and stomps his way around the large, oak table on the other side of me. We all move at once, except for Jude. I push myself away as quickly as possible, shielding my pup. The chair beneath me falls and my back hits the wall. Jude stands between his father and me. Devin has Grace pinned next to me. His back to her chest. And Vince and Veronica rise slowly and walk backward, not taking their eyes off the aggressive shifter.

This isn't how it's supposed to work. When a challenge is declared, it's done in public for the pack to witness. Jude rises and puts his arm out as though to shield me, but his father isn't moving in my direction, and I wish he'd forget about me and only think about stopping his father. They should be separated. They should be away from each other until the fight for dominance is ready to commence. My heart races as the Betas grab their Alpha's arms in an attempt to keep him back. He rips his arms from their grasp and pushes each of them away, shoving his hands against their chests. It is chaos before us, and as tears brim in my eyes, my little one cries.

The worry in Grace's eyes and the sheer fear that fills the room is my undoing.

Jude's brothers are shielding their mate. She's in complete hysterics and trying to pull them back away from their father.

"You two want to fight me as well? I'll end all of you!" He

screams at his sons who are merely shielding their fragile mate from his anger. It's obvious she's terrified for them, but she's going to get hurt. Just as the thought hits me, everything turns violent. If my back weren't cemented to this wall I'd lunge for her and pull her away, but I'd have gotten there too late. Luke, out of pure rage, slams a hard fist against his father's jaw. The sickening sound sends everything into slow motion. The Alpha's arm raises and he shifts his hand, the claws extending and shining as they sharpen before my eyes.

"No!" Emma screams squeezing between her two mates and turning her body, her back to the Alpha to push Luke out of the way. Half of her body in front of Luke and half in front of Owen. She's foolish to think she could do anything other than put herself into harm's way, which is exactly what she's done. Her shove doesn't do anything to move Luke, and Owen isn't quick enough to pull her small body away. Their father's claws smack Luke's chin and then lands hard against Emma's cheek, splitting the skin and slamming her small body onto the table.

Veronica lunges across the table and reaches for Emma. But the vampire is slow. I've seen vampires before. They've recently come more and more to Shadow's camp. Their movements are far too fast for my eyes to track, nearly a blur of jerky movements. Veronica's speed is absent; she moves no quicker than any of us would.

At first I feel a hint of betrayal and nearly push myself away from the wall to grab the human myself, but then I see her own shock and hear Vince's breath hitch as he races to be alongside his mate. Veronica's eyes widen with fear as she recognizes her failed efforts. Her breath stalls and she frantically pushes her upper body across the table in an effort to reach Emma as she slowly slips off the table. I don't understand. Nothing is as it should be. Veronica barely catches Emma's small hand, struggling to pull her unconscious and limp body across the table. Vince climbs on the table and pulls Emma across to safely shield her from the snarling werewolves.

Her limp legs smack against the chair as Vince pushes her body to Devin. Devin's grip on his own mate is harsh as he pulls her behind him. The air is thick with tension as loud growls rip through the air.

"Alpha!" The Betas yell out and try to pull the crazed man back from attacking his sons. A commotion of fury and confusion grows outside the door as several loud knocks beat against the frame. It's a trap. My pup's wail is lost in the commotion as I desperately wish it would all end. Devin moves to the door and slams it shut as someone tries to enter. Jude pulls Owen's shoulder with both of his hands and Owen attempts to shift. Luke has already shifted into a stunning white wolf and his jaws have locked around his father's forearm.

All hell has broken lose. A fire of fear races through my blood.

"I'll kill you all!" The Alpha sneers as he attempts to shift, but Jude slams his fists into his father's chest, pushing him backward. His arm is ripped from Luke's jaws, spraying dark red blood; it splatters across Jude's chest and the table. Their father lands hard on the ground and rises quickly as a gray beast. He snarls, exposing his fangs and lunges at Luke. Jude shifts and circles the two wolves. Waiting for a moment to strike. Owen shifts as well but struggles to find an opening to safely attack without harming his brother.

My focus is taken from the unbearable sight as Devin's body is shoved forward from the door being pushed violently open by the heavy shoulders of several men. The Betas run past us, on our side of the table to prevent the intruders from interfering. "Challenge!" It's the only word that registers on my left through all the screams suffocating the air. Men and women crowd the doorway, but don't dare to enter more than a few feet. Their eyes wide with the same fear that churns my gut.

Jude. Tears flow easily as all I can do is watch.

The two wolves, one white and one gray, spar with the desire to kill, snarling and biting into each other's bodies. Luke whimpers as his father clamps his jaws around Luke's back leg.

Jude's wolf, a dark brown, monster of a wolf, attacks. He grips his father's exposed throat easily in his jaws and clamps hard, digging his fangs into the flesh. But he doesn't strike to kill. It's a warning. His father doesn't budge and instead a loud snap sounds through the room. Luke's wolf howls in pain as his leg breaks. Owen's wolf snarls and lunges for the leg of his father on a path of justified vengeance. A low growl resonates through the room from the dark brown wolf, halting Owen's attack. The growl is one meaning death will come if he's not obeyed. Their father slowly loosens his hold on Luke and the wounded wolf limps in pain. Owen runs to be at his brother's side. He pushes his side against the white wolf, leading him closer to us, closer to safety.

Jude growls again and the sound is meant to be obeyed. My blood rushes with adrenaline as the room goes silent. Waiting for his father to submit or die. My vision is obstructed by the large table, and I find myself slowly walking close and leaning against the table to look at Jude's father. The wolf's eyes are crazed and his lip is curled back, revealing his fangs covered in blood.

He arches his neck feigning submission, and I can practically see the decision to trick Jude forming in his sick mind. Everything plays in slow motion before me and I haven't the time to warn Jude. As his neck goes limp, Jude loosens his grip on his father and takes a cautious step back. The wolf continues to lay, surprising me. His eyes spark of fury. The room is so quiet that the sound of Jude's paw settling in a small pool of blood is easily heard. And then the snarl from his father tears through the silence. But instead of attacking

Jude, the wolf leaps off the ground and lunges for me.

My blood rushes hot as I scream and push my weight backward. Devin's strong arm wraps around my waist, pulling me back as Jude leaps in the air, jaws open, and clamps around his father's neck. They both land heavy on the table. I continue screaming and holding my crying baby closer to me as Jude rips his father's throat out in front of me, in front of everyone. His wolf continues to claw against the dead wolf as a dark pool of blood spills down his fur and soaks into the table.

The only other sounds I'm vaguely aware of as I rock my body and try to calm myself and my son are the sounds of murmuring and then silence. It only lasts a small moment before I peek up at the sound of clothes ruffling as everyone in the room kneels and then bows. With all of the adrenaline still racing through me and my head clouded by the visions of what's just happened, it's hard to believe it's over. That it ended just as quickly as it began.

Jude's wolf calms and paces on the table, staring at the Betas who have kneeled and lowered their heads. He shifts with his back to me. His muscles ripple and glisten with sweat as he wipes his face with the back of his hand. I stare at the blood on his hand as he turns, taking in all the people bowing before him. My baby finally calms, still making small sounds of irritation, as I continue to rock and pat his back. I feel distant; the shock makes my body tremble.

As his eyes land on me, I realize I haven't bowed to him. I'm the only one not on my knees and my mouth falls open in horror. My hand leaves my son's back and cradles his head to me, and I quickly attempt to kneel. I swallow thickly, feeling his eyes bore into me as he jumps off the table, landing on both feet directly in front of me. I try to lower my head in submission, but his hand cups my chin and brings my eyes to his.

"You will never bow to me." My lips part in shock as his handsome face leans down as he kisses the crook of my neck. I close my eyes and breathe in his masculine scent, knowing exactly why he's kissing me there. As I look into Jude's eyes, our son wiggles in my arms. It's hard to miss that all eyes are on us. Jude's hand curves around the baby's head and he leans down to give him a small kiss.

Jude looks me in the eyes and says, "Don't you ever put yourself into danger again." The admonishment nearly has my knees buckling under me. His dominance radiates off him and my body involuntarily shakes. His arm wraps around my waist and pulls me closer to him. He whispers in the hot air between us, "You scared me." His soft lips press against mine. "I never want you two in danger ever again."

My shoulders collapse inward and I fall against his chest. With one hand stroking my back and the other holding my son, Jude leans down and kisses each of us again.

CHAPTER 12

JUDE

None of the emotion has dimmed inside of me. I can't believe she'd tempt fate like that. My wolf's fear of seeing her in danger is still very much present. I've never known fear like that. The very idea that she could be harmed ... it brings me to my knees. I never want to feel that again. I lean down and give my mate and our son a kiss and do my best to calm myself. My shoulders bristle and inside my wolf continues to howl.

My brothers are the same. Although their mate is far more wounded than my own.

She's up and conscious but being human is really going to take a toll on her healing. I can't help but to feel guilty. Had I known how fucked my father had become, I never would've stood for bringing our mates. With my shoulders rising and falling heavily, I resist accepting that what's done is done. None of it feels real and yet, with the bond pulsing in my blood, I know damn well this is what fate has brought us all.

I catch Owen's eye and speak through our bond, "Is she all right?"

"No, she's too fucking stubborn." A moment passes before he lets out a breath and offers a nod. "She'll be all right." A small smile plays at my lips. They both dote over her, and she pushes them away, assuring them she's fine. The cut on her cheek looks pretty bad, but a healer will make sure she doesn't scar. Owen shakes his head. "She'll be fine."

"I wish she'd fucking listen."

I hear Devin snort and then respond to Luke. "You and me both." Although his arm is wrapped around Grace's waist casually, it's all too apparent she's shaken. Everyone in the room is, yet there's a sense of peace in its finality.

Looking between Devin and Luke as the conversation continues, I realize we've all bonded over this. It's not unheard of for several Alphas to bond, but it is extremely rare.

The realization is slow to wash over me, as I take in the room of faces that seem familiar and all of them watching us.

I'm Alpha of this pack now. I challenged and killed my father. A cold sweat breaks out along my skin. I didn't mean for this to happen. I look around the room and watch as the Betas clean the mess I left of my father. We'll build him a pyre and bury him as an Alpha should be buried. A sickness churns in my stomach. What have I done? It's impossible for me to know what I've set into motion and what will come next for us.

"Do you want us to stay for a while?" Devin's question disrupts my thoughts. I struggle to respond. I'm not sure I want this at all. I look around the room again and recognize nearly every face. My heart clenches. I only wanted to save them from a horrible decision my father made, but I wasn't prepared to lead them myself.

"You know when I first saw you, I wondered how long it would take for you to join my pack." I stare back at Devin. His hand comes down on my shoulder. "And then I got to know you and I started wondering when you were going to leave." I place my hand on his shoulder and squeezed. He tells me, "You are meant to be an Alpha."

Words escape me and I don't know what to say, so I say nothing. I pull him in for a quick hug, making sure to hit him hard on the back so we don't look like pussies.

"Alpha." Leon comes up to us and it takes me a moment to realize he's talking to me.

A grim look crosses his face and I immediately straighten my back. "What is it?"

"We had a planned visit this afternoon. They'll be here soon."

"With who?"

"The vampires."

I repress my snarl. "Will I have the pleasure of meeting Victor as well?" The old man I owe my life to finally smirks.

"No, not today. Hopefully by ending this pact with them, we'll never have to see him again." A look of terror crosses his face before he quickly adds, "If that's your intention, Alpha."

I grip his shoulder, just as Devin gripped mine. "I'm not my father, Leon. I'll always want your opinion. The opinion of the pack matters to me." At those words I realize I have yet to even meet my pack. When I was younger it was relatively large, six families altogether.

"I appreciate that Alpha; I don't want you to think I would challenge your decision."

I swallow thickly and ask him plainly, "Is there anyone here who would like to challenge me?" The thought gives me mixed feelings. On one hand, I could easily hand the pack over to someone worthy and avoid the responsibility. On the other hand, I know I could lead this pack and be an Alpha they deserve.

Leon shakes his head as Marcellus walks up from behind us and interrupts. "We've been waiting for you to come back, Jude."

"Alpha, the pack has been assembled." I nod my head at Marcellus and take a deep breath, looking around the room one last time. A single moment, only minutes, has changed so many lives forever more.

CHAPTER 13

VERONICA

I lean against my mate as Jude makes his way past each of the members of his pack in the field in front of the main cabin. The air is cleansing and the breeze welcome. The stench of blood still billows from the front doors. Knowing so little of inner pack dynamics, I watch with curiosity. He recognizes most of them and they greet him with a warmth my coven never would. It seems natural that he should be their Alpha. The whispers agree. I hear them all, although so much fainter now than before.

It's a shame what's happened to his father. His mental health had been slowly declining for months. Ever since the sorcerer came. The thought of Victor makes me stiffen and

Vince holds me tighter. I peer up at him and there's nothing but concern in his eyes. He knows and there's so much to tell him, but not now. My body shudders and chills as I try to listen once again in the crowded room. It's as though my hearing is waning and that makes me more than uncomfortable.

Lately my abilities have been slipping. It's an odd feeling, as is the fear of the unknown. I knew what I was risking when I took that drug, but I wish I knew more about what to expect. Vince's arm stays possessively wrapped around me and I cling to his arm with both hands. I force myself not to look back up at him and into his emotion-filled gaze. I know it's because of what happened today. I felt his fear.

I swallow thickly and push my body against his, knowing it will calm him. He's not taking the changes well. And if I'm honest, I'm not either. I have moments of regret. But I keep the big picture in mind. Giving into the tired pull, I lay my cheek against his chest. I want a full life with my mate, and maybe soon I'll be a version of a mortal that will be with him. He knows that when he is gone, I don't intend to stay on this Earth. I only want to live so long as my mate lives. He leans down and kisses my hair. Just as I settle into his embrace, relaxed and at peace, I hear a dreadful sound. Vampires.

I hiss and gain the unwanted attention from the pack. Although the looks vary, Jude gives me his full attention and that's all that's needed. "You're expecting visitors, Jude?" I attempt to right myself and push my mate just slightly away.

He doesn't let up though and I can't blame him.

"They're here?"

"I can faintly hear them, maybe a mile or two away."

Jude directs his pack to leave and to stay within their homes while Devin's pack, Jude's brothers, and the Betas gather around him.

"I want you to go inside." My eyes widen at Vince's whispered words.

"I will not."

He murmurs, his lips nearly touching my ears, "You are not well."

"I'll be fine." I seethe through my teeth. I won't be shut away. Even if I am becoming mortal. The air leaves my lungs as I fear Vince will treat me differently once I'm mortal, but I quickly let go of unwanted emotion. I square my shoulders and regain my composure. "I will not hide." After a long moment he nods but pulls me closer to his side. I suppose I'll settle for this compromise. Besides, I love my place at his side. I love him more than I have ever loved myself.

As soon as the car nears, I know exactly what coven they're from. I recognize them instantly. Adreana's going to be pissed her sister coven is taking the side of the traitors. They're fucking idiots for believing the Authority had anything to do with the tainted blood.

As the three vampires park the Porsche and shut their doors, they look around at the gathering of wolves feigning little interest, but I can hear racing hearts from the Betas that greet them. I notice that Jude stays back, and Devin closes the distance between them. Staying behind Jude. I have to turn to see that Grace stays back and beside Lena and her little one. My eyes rest on the small bundle and my hand subconsciously lowers. I've wanted for only two things all my life, and fate may have given me both if only in exchange for my immortality.

"We have an appointment." Demetri is the first to speak and my attention is drawn back to the open field. I've met him a time or two. He's a vicious vampire and hasn't learned any discipline in the hundred or so years that he's lived. His queen is spoiled, and she allows her coven to do whatever the fuck they want. I've never been a fan of hers.

One of the Betas speak, I haven't a clue what their names are. "There's been a rearrangement of power in the pack." Jude crosses the distance and Devin stays just behind him. "We have a new Alpha now." Jude steps in front of the Beta and extends his hand as a formality. Demetri takes too fucking long looking at the offered hand before he finally shakes it. It's an insult. Jude takes it in stride, simply smirking.

"I believe your presence is unnecessary at this time."

"Unnecessary? You no longer back our coven?" His eyes narrow and the other two vampires walk quickly to Demetri's side; as they do, Devin, Luke and Owen stand beside Jude, shoulder to shoulder. There are only three vampires, there's no doubt in my mind that they'll simply sulk back to their coven. But still, I'm uneasy watching them size each other up.

"I will not lead my pack into war against the Authority." Jude's voice is calm, even, and loud enough for all to hear. It's fucking effective as well. The vampires lose their composure with expressions of shock and disgust as they realize Jude is serious. I huff a laugh at their loss. Demetri's dark eyes meet mine as he hears the laughter. I didn't mean for him to hear it and I should've kept my mouth shut and stayed in the background. I don't want to face vampires at the moment when I'm so uneasy with my own state of immortality. It's easy to see that he recognizes me, just as I did him.

"You? You take the side of these dogs?" A low growl resonates from Vince's massive chest. I turn to him on my tiptoes and nip his neck in admonishment. I hate that he gives them any of his emotions. "How could you side with them? You're one of the elites!" I don't react to Demetri's rage and the contempt in his voice. I merely spear my hands through my hair and lean against my mate.

"I'm quite comfortable with how things are Demetri." In a flash, the vampires surround us. Again, I ignore them. I act as though I'm not threatened. But I'm a liar. I'm frighteningly aware of how weak I am as a mortal and I'm desperate for my powers to return. But I'd be a fool to try them out right now. I don't want them to know. Demetri stands directly in front of us and the two fools pace around us.

"Back down vampire." Jude's hard voice breaks through the tension. "We have no use for the alliance with your queen. You can tell her the truce is off with a new Alpha having taken power and we will not back her in the war."

The vampires sneer at Jude. "She will be highly displeased."

"She should reconsider her decision. The Authority is not responsible for the poisoned blood."

"They sold it to us." As Demetri speaks his hand flies out and comes exceptionally close to my face. I gasp and attempt to move back. But I'm slow. Although he doesn't hit me, my lack of speed is noticed by everyone.

Demetri takes a step closer to me and Vince doesn't waste a second to pound his hard fists against Demetri's chest, sending him backward to land on his ass. The power radiates and instantly, the werewolves gather. Demetri rises up in a blur and tilts his head to examine me, completely unaffected by Vince's warning to steer clear of me. "What have you done to her?"

"They've done nothing." I scowl and expose my fangs to the intrusive vampire, but he can tell. The air around me has changed.

"This is why the Authority must fall. You're not thinking clearly."

"Me?" My dark eyes widen with fury. "Did you see their Alpha?" I hate that I'm allowing him to get the best of me. I attempt to school my features. "He wasn't thinking clearly."

"How much of that blood did you drink, dear Veronica?" Demetri smirks at me as though he has everything all figured out.

"None. I drink from my mate." My fingers play along Vince's neck. "I wanted this; I took the drug because I wanted more than this life."

"You're an idiot to give up your immortality. My queen will—"

"Enough!" Vince's large hand wraps around the vampire's neck and squeezes. The vampire's hands fly to his neck.

"Leave now." Jude snarls into Demetri's ear and Vince drops the vampire, who quickly backs away in jerked, blurred motions. He stumbles and struggles to breathe but after a shared look of contempt between him and Jude, the vampires leave.

"It's all but certain they'll return," one of the Betas says to Jude.

He shares a look with them, and I have no idea what he says, but I know there's much to be done to keep this pack safe from the war ahead.

CHAPTER 14

LENA

All I want is my mate. Ever since I felt the pull to him, I've felt unsteady without him by my side. There's a comfort when I think of him, it's even stronger when I see him, but I am desperate for his touch. He glances back at me and I now know what a mate's pull is. My heart races and I turn only once to check on my pup one last time.

I don't want to leave him, but I know I have to do this for Jude. Both women were extremely willing to watch him. More than willing. They've been trying to take him from me every moment they could for the last few nights that we've been in Gray Mountain. Four days have passed since Jude's become Alpha and the transition has been seamless. At least for Jude it has been. I'm still getting used to the new faces. At least I have Devin and his pack here for the moment. They've decided to stay as guests, no doubt also for protection.

I can tell both Veronica and Grace are a bit jealous of Lizzie's pregnancy. Not in a malicious way, but they both want to give their mates young. I can't blame them. Every time I see Jude holding our son, I want to have a dozen more.

I'm not in heat, so I doubt tonight will bring more young. But he will claim me under the full moon, and I will be the Alpha mate the seers foretold. A chill goes through my body as I walk alongside Jude. I'm not sure I'm ready for this. I don't know that I'll ever feel ready, but I want nothing more than to be his, so I'm willing to let him claim me tonight.

It's not enough that I feel the pull to him. I know I need to let him claim me. My fingertips glide over the small indents in my neck. Where I was first bitten and claimed by Shadow. My body trembles remembering the pain. Not just from the claiming, but from giving myself to him. I gave him far too much. I push the thoughts away, not liking the memories gathering. Jude takes my hand in his and I squeeze his hand, needing his confidence and his strength.

Touched by the glow of the moon as we walk out to a clearing in a distant, protected woods, Jude pulls me closer. He brings my knuckles to his lips and gives them a kiss before stopping us in front of a large group of willow trees. He pulls back the hobble branches and I duck to move under them with him. The soft leaves brush against my skin and give me goosebumps. His hand grazes along my shoulder and the small curve of my waist as I stand in the opening of the willows. The sight is breathtaking. We're in a circular clearing surrounded by trees and sweet honeysuckle. The grass is lush and nearly a soft cushion beneath our feet. The bright white of the full moon shines down and illuminates the natural beauty surrounding us.

"It's beautiful." I whisper the words, almost too afraid to speak and disrupt the picturesque surroundings.

He murmurs at the shell of my ear, sending a needy warmth to flow down my shoulders and pebble my nipples. "Not as beautiful as you." Without waiting for a response, his large hand cups my chin and brings my lips to his. His soft lips against mine steal the breath from my lungs. He gently nips my bottom lip, making me part for him. His hot tongue dances with mine as his hand deftly unzips my dress. He lets it fall to a pool of fabric at my feet and pulls back to look at my body. His half-hooded eyes roam my body and light with lust. "So fucking beautiful." I blush at his words and smile as he opens his pants, all the while his eyes stay on me and my heart races.

We both stand naked in front of each other, ready to bare ourselves to one another and fortify our bond under the power of the full moon. I'm ready to let him claim me as his. Truly his. This is what was always meant to be. My fingers run along his jaw, loving the scratch of his stubble. I close my eyes as he kisses the crook of my neck and lifts my body easily before gently laying me under him. His large, muscular frame cages me in. I lay breathless under him as he parts my legs and moves his fingers to my clit. My head falls back as his blissful touch shoots a numbing pleasure to my core. He licks and kisses my neck, and the sensation is linked with the throbbing need in my aching heat. He doesn't let up, between the soft kisses and forceful touch. I moan for him and let the pleasure distract me from what's to come.

"Come for me baby." My pussy pulses at his command, sending a wild wave of shudders to paralyze my body. My body trembles as I whimper helplessly under his relentless touch. He draws out my orgasm and I nearly push him away from the intensity. With my body trembling, he readjusts and I'm all too aware that the time has come.

His hard, chiseled chest presses down on me slightly as he pushes the head of his dick at my hot entrance. "Good girl, hot and wet for your mate." A wave of arousal wets my core even more at his words.

My fingers spear in his hair and I pull his lips to mine with a desperation I've never felt before. He moans into my mouth as he moves slowly, deeper and deeper inside of me. I gasp as he stretches my walls with a hint of pain that only adds to the pleasure. My legs wrap around his hips and my heels dig into his muscular ass as he flexes, pumping agonizingly slow, shallow thrusts into my heat. Each thrust pushes more of him inside of me. I moan and writhe, thinking I won't be able to take him all. He hits against my wall with each pump, making me grip onto his shoulders and bite his neck to keep the screams of pleasures from escaping. Another orgasm rips through my body, quickly heating and numbing my core. It's too intense and not enough all at the same time.

"Yes! Bite me baby." At his words and quickening pace, I sink my teeth deeper into his flesh. His thrusts become hard and deep, each one jolting my body against the ground. Fuck, he feels so good. I'm lost in the pleasure of him. I've never wanted more in my life than to have more of him in every way for as long as I live. He brings me to the edge of yet another orgasm and I find myself desperate to hold onto him. I feel as though I'm falling as a blinding light flashes before my eyes. A sharp pinch makes me gasp as his teeth bite into the mark on the left side of my neck. I grip onto him as the pain is washed away by wave after wave of pleasure. The tides come in slow and threatening as they overwhelm my body. My body begs to thrash under him, but I'm paralyzed, gently shaking beneath him.

He bites me again and again. Rutting into me wildly with his own desperation. My back digs into the dirt as he snarls against my neck and fucks into me mercilessly. My own teeth dig deeper into his neck and the metallic taste of his blood filters into my mouth. I whimper as he thrusts into me brutally, biting into my neck again. Tears form in the corner of my eyes as he savagely ruins Shadow's mark. I have no doubt that Shadow's claim to me, the scar, will be completely unrecognizable. And although I can feel the slight pain over the overwhelming pleasure buzzing through every part of my body, I love the fact that it's destroyed. I love that Jude has ruined it.

I love that he is taking me for himself.

He pulls away from my neck and the move makes me release him as well. He stares down at me as he shoves himself deep inside and stills as I tremble under him. My blunt nails dig into his shoulders as I cry out his name. His eyes never leave mine. They shine with love and possession.

"Mine." He leans down and kisses me with passion and desire. He pounds into me again and again before kissing the right side of my neck. My body heats to an impossible temperature as he kisses the crook of my neck and lights every nerve in my body aflame.

"Yes!" I scream out as my pussy spasms around his cock. He growls low and deep and it's the sexiest fucking sound I've ever heard. And then he does it. He bites the crook of my neck and holds me down as he pulses deep inside me with his own release.

My body flames with love and completion. My mate, my Alpha has claimed me. My lips part as I struggle to breathe. My chest swells and my body trembles as he releases me. His strong arms lift his body above mine. His eyes focus on his mark as a slow smile grows on his face. My heart softens and I relax on the ground beneath him, feeling proud that I've given him this. He deserves every piece of me and I of him. Life has kept us apart for too long.

Just as the thought hits me, the burning starts. I wince and try to avoid showing pain. I can't disappoint him. I don't want him to see how weak I am, but the pain grows and my hands fly to my neck. One on each side. Tears well and I start to thrash as it radiates down my shoulders in sharp stinging lightning pains. Jude pushes my hand away and I involuntarily fight him, feeling the need to get away from his hot touch, but he pins me down. His tongue laps at the marks on the left side and a wave of cooling relief flows down that side of my body. As I start to plead for relief on the other side, he moves to the right and gently licks the wound. My chest rises and falls with surrender as he moves back and forth, licking and kissing my neck. He doesn't stop, not until the shocking heat has nearly vanished.

I wrap my arms around him and close my eyes as the chill of his touch eases the pain, leaving only the slight aftershocks of pleasure to lull me into deep relaxation. All at once, my body feels heavy and swayed by the moon. My eyes fall with exhaustion. "I love you, Jude," I whisper into his ear before kissing his neck.

"I love you, Lena." The last words I hear as I fall into a deep and much needed sleep are "my love; my mate."

CHAPTER 15

LENA

The little yawn JJ gives me as I pat his bottom and he rests his sleeping head on my shoulder melts my heart. We decided on Jeremiah James, but JJ for short. Jude's eyes lit up at the nickname when I asked him. The memory fills me with warmth; every small thought of my mate does. I'd hoped that he would love it and I wasn't disappointed at all by his reaction.

The soft pat pat is in time with my body as I gently rock and shush him with the warmth of the sun coming through the open window in the great room of the main cabin. In only a month, this place has changed so much. Jude and his brothers gave me and Emma creative control... which I fully handed off to Emma. I'm growing to love her and the pack. She actually helped me come up with JJ's name. For the first time in so long I can truly say I have a family and that I'm a member of a pack. Truly and in every way. As is my little pup.

Jude's connection with JJ is undeniable. Although everyone knows JJ isn't Jude's biological son, he's accepted by the pack as his. Never in my life did I think I could feel this way. There's nothing but warmth and welcome from everyone surrounding us. For once, my heart is open and that scares me more than anything. When I'm closed off, I at least have armor. But here, I can't be guarded. The feeling of belonging is far too overwhelming.

I don't doubt that there's spittle and drool all over the top of this beautiful dress Jude gave me. It's made of pale, pink chiffon and ends just above my knees. He said he loves the way the color makes my skin glow. I happen to think it's Jude who makes me glow, and Emma and Grace agree, but I keep that little tidbit from my mate.

JJ coos and I rub my cheek against his soft little head and inhale deeply. Babies have this smell that makes me flush with happiness and a sense of peace. I rest my cheek gently on him and hum softly as Jude continues his conversation with Devin. I haven't been paying attention to what they're talking about, but the loud bark of laughter from Jude and the playful slap from Grace onto Devin's arm makes me happy. A bright smile lights quickly across my face.

I can't believe this is my pack. We're sheltered and safe with Devin and his pack surrounding us, but they're leaving soon and this morning's meeting has been all about the details of the packs' union. Even Reece and Addy have bonded to both packs although they'll stay with us. Together we're stronger, so we shall remain imprinted. I'm not ready for them to go, though. We're protected here, but it's not about that. It's more the simple fact that I'll miss them. No matter how much Grace promises they'll visit, I don't want them to leave.

Jude must sense my anxiety, because the moment my heart starts to race with worry and trepidation, his large arm wraps around my waist and pulls me into his warmth. My wolf rubs against my side, closest to our mate. She loves the way our bodies press together. She pushes against his hard body and the act calms me. I feel nothing but at peace in his embrace. The approving rumble that vibrates through him stirs my wolf and makes my heart swell with devotion.

As I settle in his embrace, my eyes find an older woman resting against the side wall. Her gray hair has streaks of white in it and thick wire-framed glasses shield her pale blue eyes. A small smile slowly grows on her face. As she walks toward us, I expect my wolf's hackles to raise or for her to whimper in fear, instead she stretches lazily and rests sweetly against my side once again.

Jude kisses my hair and whispers in my ear. "You look

beautiful, baby." His warm breath makes me wriggle away as it tickles the crook of my neck. His low, sexy chuckle in my ear makes me want to nip his bottom lip in admonishment and lick that dip in his throat. A wave of unexpected arousal heats my core and has me practically panting for his touch. I clear my throat, straightening and moving slightly away from him as I try to avoid concentrating on how good his hands feel on me. My heat must be coming soon. I look into my mate's eyes and wonder if we'll have another.

The older woman stops in front of us and smiles sweetly before scenting the air and cocking a brow. The knowing smirk on her lips makes me blush. But thankfully, she doesn't comment. "I just wanted to tell you both how happy I am that Jude's back." Her small, wrinkled hand pats mine. "And that he's found such a sweet mate." I can't help but to smile at her kindness.

"I'm happy to be home Marci." He bends down and gives the older woman a kiss on the cheek. A happiness clouded with a bit of grief flashes in her eyes as she pats my hand once again and then walks away.

"Who is she?" I look up at Jude and find a sad smile on his lips.

"She was my mother's friend."

"I'm sorry." I don't know what else to say. It must be very hard for him to come home after all these years. Especially given the circumstance. It's a dark tale that lacked a happily ever after, but hopefully with Jude back, we can ease the pain that came with such a tragedy.

"We aren't that far away from each other." Emma's soft voice breaks the sad moment and I'm grateful for it. "Your packs could still do that mind talking couldn't you?"

Jude huffs a deep laugh. "Too far. Way too far for that."

"So you'd lose the connection?"

Jude clucks his tongue against the roof of his mouth. "We wouldn't lose it. Not unless we break the pack bond."

Devin speaks up, "I don't have any intention of breaking our bond. Not with you and not with Luke and Owen either."

All four Alphas are a sight to behold on their own, but seeing them all at once, all in agreement is an intimidating sight. It reminds me of what the seers told me long ago. About how our pack would bond and strengthen ties to be an unstoppable force. It makes me wonder what we would need to be preventing, what we'd be fighting against. The vampires flash into mind, but they're gone instantly. It would be foolish of them to fight against us. Three strong packs aligned together and close in proximity. It would mean death to them if they even considered approaching us.

For now, there is peace, or at least a stalemate. I look down at my son and back up to my mate and hope it will stay that way. But somewhere, deep in my soul. I know it won't.

CHAPTER 16

VERONICA

MONTHS LATER....

V ince's hand travels along my belly with care. His fingertips barely touch my skin, leaving a tickle of goosebumps in his path. His silver eyes look up at me in awe as he bends to kiss my belly. I can't believe what he told me. I can't imagine it's true...after all this time. Miracles and second chances aren't meant for people like me...but then again I have Vince. "Are you sure?"

"I'm sure." He closes his eyes and rubs his nose against my belly and down lower before humming with satisfaction. "You are most certainly pregnant with my pup." His words bring a heat of love through my blood. My eyes close to push down the emotions and I lean my head against the pillow. His hands grab my hips and tilt them so he can bury his nose between my legs. A warmth of a blush travels through my chest and into my cheeks as I let out a short laugh.

"Is that why I feel so tired?" I smile wickedly as he takes a languid, hot lick down there. It's been a few days since I've taken any blood from him, but I don't hunger for it and my fangs have lost their length. It's been so long since I've indulged in fruits and breads. The taste is nothing like I remember, but it offers me some strength. Only a small portion of what I'd once had. I'd started to worry that the exhaustion was something else. That in exchange for my immortality, the drug would deliver me death. It's something that I wouldn't have minded before, but knowing what I could have with Vince, the pull of a fated mate and all the beauties of a fragile life, I want to live. I want to experience this.

He looks up at me with a grin, "If your pregnancy is like wolves, then you'll sleep all day." I'm happy he's finally smiling again. I worried him. He wasn't fooled when I started to show the signs of the drug working. I'd only taken a little, but it was enough.

"But how will I boss my dirty mutt around if I'm always asleep?" He laughs at my playful question before sucking my clit into his mouth. With a moan forced from me, I push my head deeper into the pillow as my heels dig into the mattress.

"That's right." His warm breath on my heat sends another

wave of arousal through me. "Get wet for your dirty mutt." I can feel him smile against me as he pushes his thick fingers into my pussy. He curls his fingers and hits my g-spot, the sudden sensation sends me over the edge. My body heats and numbs as waves of pleasure rock through me.

"Fuck that was quick." I barely register his words as my body trembles beneath him. He quickly pulls off his pants and settles between my legs. He doesn't hesitate to push all of himself into me. My fists twist in the sheets as my body bows. My lips part in ecstasy as he rocks into my body.

With my eyes closed, I hardly register the sound of tires squealing in the driveway. It happens so fast. My blood turns to ice and I'm unable to stop it. My eyes open and I push against Vince's heavy chest as I hear the guns being fired. In rapid succession bullets fly through the air, shattering the windows and flying past our bodies. I scream as Vince's massive frame comes down around mine, caging me in and protecting me. "Stay." His voice is strained as his cheek pushes against mine. Pleading with me to be still and quiet under him.

My heart pounds as I'm trapped and weak beneath him. Filled with nothing but terror.

The seconds drag on as our world crashes down upon us. The glass breaks and bullets spray with recklessness. Vince's body jolts as one and then another and then another bullet hits him. He winces in pain, and I try to push against him. To help him. To do something. I would give anything in this moment to protect my mate and ease him of the pain. Tears pour down my face as I try to hold back my scream.

His body sways as his eyes lose focus. I shake my head as my hands grab his face. The rough stubble brushes against my palms.

"Vince." His heavy body falls as his eyes roll back in his head. "Vince!" I scream in his face. "No! Vince!" This can't be happening. "Vince!"

I lay screaming under Vince's heavy, unconscious body. I have no strength, no speed, no immortality. I pound my fists against him. "Vince!" My throat burns as the screams are ripped from me. "Vince!"

I barely register time passing, the tires squeal again, and all I can focus on is my mate. I pound against him, begging him to wake up. My mind is a whirl of disbelief, chaos, and utter grief.

Devin storms into the room and grips Vince's heavy body, lifting him off me. "Save him!" I scream at Devin as he lays Vince on the floor. This can't be happening. My head shakes violently, denying the reality.

Tears cloud my vision. As I wipe them away, I still in fear. Clear tears, the tears of mortals. I stare back at Devin as his fingers dig into Vince's shoulder. Vince screams in agony as the bullet is pulled from his flesh. "Vince!" A glass shard digs into my knee as I crawl to him and hold onto his waist as if my life depends on his. I don't care about the physical pain, I only care about him. My body shakes as sobs are forced from my chest. "I'll kill them Vince." I swallow hard, "I'll make them pay." Vince rolls away from Devin and opens his eyes.

"Veronica." I crawl up his body and spear my fingers through his hair. I kiss him with everything I have. The salty tears coat my lips, but I don't stop kissing him. My breath comes in shallow pants as his hands press on my back and pull my body to his. My arm pushes against his chest and he winces in pain. I pull back, horrified that I've hurt him.

"It's silver." Devin's tone is deathly low and filled with concern. "We need to get him to the shed."

"But you got them out." I search the ground for the fucking bullets. "Did you get them all?"

Devin shakes his head before leaning down to gather a bullet and hold it out for me to see. It burns his hands, but he only snarls slightly from the pain as it singes his skin. "They're designed to splinter," he says.

My lips part and eyes widen as I look at the crumbling bullet between his forefinger and thumb. My poor mate.

"It's dissolving. We'll do transfusions until it's completely left his system." My body shudders as I close my eyes and let the sadness wash over me. My poor Vince will be in such agonizing pain. I nuzzle my head into his chest, letting the tears fall.

"I'll be all right, baby." Vince is barely coherent, but he pushes the words out through clenched teeth.

Who did it? Tell me you know. You have to know!" I search Devin's hard expression for something. For anything.

"We will find them. And we will destroy them. I promise you that." I nod my head in complete agreement. I will find every one of those bastards and suck the life from them.

And then I remember my mortality. I've never felt weaker in my life. I give myself a moment of regret and then my eyes harden in anger. I will make this right. I look at my wounded mate and then back to Devin. "We need to go to Alec, and we need to talk to my queen."

About the Author

Thank you so much for reading my romances. I'm just a stay at home Mom and an avid reader turned Author and I couldn't be happier.

I hope you love my books as much as I do!

More by Willow Winters
www.willowwinterswrites.com/books